THE
MIRACULOUS MILK COW

THE

Miraculous Milk Cow

*More Tales My Great Great Grandfather Might
Tell About Life in a Ghetto of Russia
in the Time of the Czars*

By

Herman I. Kantor

with Eric Larson

Illustrated by Jan Golden

FITHIAN PRESS • SANTA BARBARA, CALIFORNIA • 1994

My thanks to my fellow Villagers, who helped with suggestions; to Adam Cintz, for describing to me conditions in a small shtetl in Poland and for ideas for a story; to Florence Bernstein for help with many Yiddish expressions; and to my publisher, who has always been very helpful. Many writers like to actually hear the stories they have written, and it is helpful to me. For this help I should like to thank my wife, Ruth.

—H.K.

This is a work of fiction. Any resemblance to real events or to real persons, living or dead, is pure coincidence—no, it is a miracle.

Copyright © 1994 Herman I. Kantor
All Rights Reserved
Printed in the United States of America

Published by Fithian Press
A division of Daniel and Daniel, Publishers, Inc.
Post Office Box 1525
Santa Barbara, CA 93102

Design by Eric Larson

LIBRARY OF CONGRESS CATALOGING-IN-PUBLICATION DATA
    Kantor, Herman I.
        The miraculous milk cow : more tales my great-great-grandfather
    might tell about life in a ghetto of Russia in the time of the czars /
    Herman I. Kantor with Eric Larson.
            p. cm.
        ISBN 1-56474-094-3 (cloth). ISBN 1-56474-095-1 (ppbk)
        1. Jews—Russia—History—Fiction. I. Larson, Eric.
    II. Title.
    PS3561.A515M48   1994
    813'.54—dc20   94-5097
                                                CIP

CONTENTS

Foreword

I was strolling in a shopping mall recently and came upon a store called Imaginarium, whose bright colors and creative atmosphere immediately attracted my attention. I could see Herman Kantor very much at home there.

Herman Kantor has a gift. He uses his fertile imagination to conjure up timeless magic in his vignettes of poor and humble people, and he does so with skill and grace, warmth and sensitivity, and delightful whimsy.

These tales grow on you. In a charming fashion they transport the reader to the simpler life of the Orsha ghetto. They are easy reading, and there is no hidden message—just the good, simple, everyday life of the inhabitants of the ghetto, and Herman Kantor's imagination.

—HERBERT SHORE, ED. D.
Executive Vice President
North American Association of Jewish Homes
and Housing for the Aging
Dallas, Texas
1993

Preface

My great-great-grandfather, Rabbi Shmul ben Shlomo, lived almost two hundred years ago in the Jewish quarter, or ghetto, on the outskirts of the town of Orsha, which was then little more than a village, in what is now Byelorussia. That was a long time ago, of course, and sadly very little of his experiences have come down to me through the intervening generations. Yet I cannot shake my curiosity about what life was like back then and how it has influenced our lives today; and since few stories of my great-great-grandfather were passed down in our family, I had only one recourse: I had to make them up.

That Rabbi Shmul lived in Orsha is true; the rest is pure fiction. I and my co-author have tried as best we could to make these tales as realistic as possible, through research and consultation with the books and individuals named in the acknowledgements.

But this is not a book of history; it is a book of fantasy. It is not about politics or great trends, or even about the details of daily life in this place or that. It is about people—their aspirations and their fears, their wisdom and their foolishness, their relationships with one another, and the spirit that allows them to carry on despite life's troubles. And in this realm, wooly fiction is often truer than bald fact.

Some readers may quarrel with some of the details in these tales; for example, the rules governing the use of the mikveh varied from one community to another, and we have adopted those which suit our story best. In other cases we have knowingly played fast and loose with historical facts, and we make no apology for it. For example, the Czarina Maria Alexandrovna was a contemporary of Rabbi Shmul, but she never really had twin daughters as we claim, and she certainly never invited a Jewish physician from the ghetto to attend a royal birth.

But what of it? If we have succeeded in portraying human nature authentically and in a way that contemporary readers can understand and enjoy, and if our little white lies help them understand themselves, their fellow human beings, and their social and religious traditions a little better, we will have achieved our purpose. The rest is of little consequence.

I believe that there is a common thread that unites the lives of Jews around the world, whether they live in Orsha, America, or Japan. Though we expect oppression, laws and regulations that cause us trouble, and even occasional violence, we are all buoyed by the spirit of "Yiddishkeit," a term coined by Leo Rosten in his excellent book, *The Joys of Yiddish*. To me, Yiddishkeit means love, tolerance, prayer, obedience to G-d's laws, respect for other people, and love for our parents and teachers. It represents the Jewish way of life in all its aspects—in fiction as well as in history, in the ghetto of Orsha or anywhere else.

The life of the Jewish people in the shtetloch of

Russia and Eastern Europe may seem far from us now, but I hope these stories will show that the spirit of that life—of love, of community, of devotion, of humor, and of Yiddishkeit—are as much a part of the Jewish experience today as they always have been.

—HERMAN I. KANTOR

THE
MIRACULOUS MILK COW

More tales my great-great-grandfather might tell
about life in a ghetto of Russia
in the time of the czars

The Two Lovers

IN CZARIST RUSSIA of the nineteenth century, almost all Jews lived in ghettos like the one in the shtetl called Orsha in central Russia. The official population of Orsha was around three thousand—the Russians who lived in town. But there were also five hundred or so Jews living in the ghetto, including my great-great-grandfather, Shmul ben Shlomo, who was the rabbi. Jews were not considered citizens of Russia, but were tolerated by the "generous mercy of his highness, the czar," or so the Russian authorities assured the Jews. Yet the ghettoites found the czars' mercy less than generous, when they found any at all, and they avoided the government and its agents like the plague. Any contact with the authorities, they feared, would result in serious complications, with someone jailed, fined, killed, or maybe all three. Therefore, whenever a dispute arose among the ghettoites, whenever a family found itself in dire straits, or when anyone was caught in a moral quagmire, they turned not to the czars' courts for justice—for what justice had they ever received from the czars?—but went instead to their local rabbi, whose advice was golden, and whose word was to them as law.

So it was that, in addition to presiding at holiday and shabbes services, my great-great-grandfather, Rabbi Shmul, also heard all the problems and troubles of the Orsha ghetto. As a result, he was loved and respected by all for his deep sympathy, his sturdy sense of fairness, and his wise judgment—which, to his congregants at least, was unerring. During his tenure as the ghetto's civic and spiritual leader, many fascinating incidents came before him, and that is how he was called upon to solve the problem of the two lovers.

In the Orsha ghetto there lived a hard-working man named Bessel ben Balta. Reb Bessel was a plumber, and was gifted with a talent few could match. A short, stocky bear of a young man, Reb Bessel could often be seen waddling from job to job, his pockets bulging with tools of his trade, many of which he had invented himself. His days were filled with the water pipes, stove pipes, and steam pipes of the ghetto homes and small factories, and he also served the village in repairing its ancient watercourses. His reputation became so widely known that even the gentile people in Orsha proper often called on him when it came to a problem of plumbing. Reb Bessel was an expert, a brain surgeon among plumbers.

Reb Bessel was still unmarried, and busy though he was, he had a deep desire to find a bride and begin a family of his own. It was with this aim that he went to Reb Sigala and asked if he might visit with his daughter, Hannah. She was a lovely girl, considered the beauty of the ghetto. She had bright, cerulean eyes that brought memories of the cloudless skies of spring; her hair was long and golden, and when she wore it up it looked like the crown of a queen. And when she favored a young man with her smile, he felt as if he had won a prize at the fair. She was everything Reb Bessel could desire.

Unfortunately, despite his skill, industry, and ample means, Reb Bessel was not everything Reb Sigala could have wanted in a son-in-law. For while Hannah was very tall, almost two meters in height, Bessel was less than a meter and a half tall—practically a midget.

Nevertheless, Reb Sigala recognized Bessel's industry and enterprise, and acquiesced to the meeting—with conditions. First, they must have a chaperone. This was standard practice in the ghetto; a young man and woman never met alone. Second, they must under no circumstances speak of marriage until their fathers had agreed and had consulted Sarah the shadchen, who would make all the arrangements for the betrothal and wedding.

This was the inviolable custom of the ghetto. One of the fathers—usually of the bride, but sometimes of the groom—would broach the subject of marriage with the other father. With great tact and lots of beating around the bush, he would let drop the suggestion that his son or daughter was of marriageable age. If the other father seemed amenable, the first would contact the shadchen to arrange the details—the dowry, preparations at the shul, and advertisement of the good news throughout the ghetto. Although there were many marriages arranged between the parents and the shadchen, often without the future bride and groom ever having met at all, it would have been an unthinkable breach of etiquette to plan a wedding without the assistance of the shadchen.

And so, with their fathers' permission, the young couple met, and it was only a few weeks later that Bessel notified his father that he wanted to marry Hannah. Reb Balta met with Reb Sigala, and they agreed to the marriage. Then they asked Sarah, the shadchen of the Orsha ghetto, to complete the arrangements for the happy day.

But no one thought to ask Hannah. That was not the custom. When her father told her she was to marry Bessel, she burst into hot tears of humiliation. Bessel was so short, she would feel ridiculous towering over him whenever they appeared together, and she could not imagine a life of continuous stooping and bending. She sobbed for long hours in her room. The wedding would be a travesty; why, the chuppa, the ceremonial canopy under which they would exchange vows, would mock them. Bessel would look like a dwarf unless the chuppa were lowered for him; but then Hannah and the rabbi would have to kneel throughout the ceremony. And what of married life? Bessel was so short he would have to stand on his toes to kiss or embrace his new wife—more than that was unthinkable.

Hannah begged her father to reconsider. How could he expect her to love a man half her height? Did he care nothing for her happiness? But her father was adamant. He had already made his decision, the shadchen had made her arrangements, and that was that.

🕮

At the same time, there lived in the ghetto a young man named Ezek ben Yussel, the son of the ghetto shames whom everyone called Drayzuch. Ezek was a handsome young man, broad of shoulder, square of jaw, and considerably taller than most of the young men his age. In his childhood he had been the natural leader of all the children's games, and he had also distinguished himself in school, where he proved to be very bright indeed. The other children looked up to him like an older brother, and it was always he who decided what game to play, where the children might go exploring, and it was usually he who broke up their fights and mediated their petty squabbles.

At age fifteen, Ezek had been apprenticed to Nathan, the tailor. Ezek helped Nathan with deliveries, and in the shop he did some of the hemming, pressing, and such. But he often talked about new ways he had thought of to do this or that, suggestions never adopted by Nathan because they made little sense. Some of Ezek's suggestions were downright silly, like his idea that you could iron two shirts at once by folding them carefully together. Nathan seldom even bothered to respond to Ezek's suggestions. The boy would never make a good tailor, and Nathan told Ezek's father so again and again. But Ezek was confident not only that he would take over Nathan's business someday, but that all the ghetto folk and even many of the town Russians would come to him for their clothes.

When Ezek turned twenty, Shames Drayzuch began to discuss finding him a bride and considering which family they might ask to make this alliance. But Shames Drayzuch hadn't even had a chance to drop a hint to anyone when Ezek made his own desires known.

"Father," he said one evening, "there is a girl in the ghetto who is more beautiful than any other. Her eyes are bright blue, and her hair is as gold as the crown of a queen. Father, I want to marry Reb Sigala's daughter, Hannah!"

Both his father and mother were shocked. Everyone in the ghetto already knew that Hannah was to be married to Bessel—Sarah the shadchen had made sure of that.

"You know Hannah is spoken for," scolded Reb Drayzuch. "How can you even think of interfering like this? Have you no shame?"

"But, Father," protested Ezek, "Bessel is unfit to marry Hannah. He's practically a dwarf, Father. They look silly together, and everyone knows it. I've spoken to Hannah already; she came into the tailor shop only yesterday. She's embarrassed to be seen with that shrimp Bessel, she told me so herself. She said she could never obey him as a wife, much less love him. She's in love with me, Father, and I'm in love with her. You're the shames; all you have to do is speak to her father and her engagement to Bessel will be withdrawn. Let dwarfs marry dwarfs, but let me marry Hannah."

Reb Drayzuch was horrified. How could his son make such an outrageous suggestion? And how could he have been so irresponsible as to discuss his marriage himself, with the girl even, and without a chaperone, yet! How could the shames propose such a thing to Hannah's father? Never before in the history of the ghetto had a marriage agreement been broken once it had been announced by the shadchen. Think of the scandal! What kind of neighbor would he be? What kind of Jew? It was unthinkable! And what was this "love" business his son was carrying on about? Marriage was supposed to be an alliance of families, a consolidation of resources and lives; since when did "love" have anything to do with it?

Of course, there was some truth to what Ezek said. Bessel and Hannah did look ridiculous together; and the shames knew it was true that Hannah did not want to marry Bessel. The more he thought about it, the more his common sense began to sway him away from strict adherence to custom.

So one afternoon Shames Drayzuch screwed up all his courage and went to see not the girl's father, Reb Sigala, but Bessel's father, Reb Balta, to sound him out. He called at Balta's home, and on the pretext of needing some plumbing done at the shul, let the conversation wander to Bessel. Then he slipped in the subject of marriage.

"So," he said as casually as he could, "I hear your son is to be married, nu?"

Reb Balta sighed deeply. "Yes, it's true. And it should be a happy thing, no? But it's not, I'm afraid; not at all. My wife and I thought about how nice it would be to be related to Sigala's family, and my son is delirious with the thought of marrying Hannah. But...." Balta looked at the ground between his feet. "For some reason, she doesn't want to marry him; she says they won't be compatible. Shames, what's with these young people? What is this 'compatible?' He's a man, she's a woman, and they're both Jewish, so what's not compatible? I don't get it at all, and now I wish the whole thing had never come up. We've already made all the arrangements with Sarah, but I'm afraid this might turn out very badly. And now it seems there is nothing to be done."

Then Reb Drayzuch told his old friend of his own son's desire to marry Hannah. "He says he's 'in love,' whatever that means, and what's more, he's already spoken to the girl—vey is mir!—and she's 'in love' with him too. Oy, what is with the kids these days? Balta, my friend, what can we do?"

And so, although it was completely against ghetto precedent, the two fathers went together to the home of Hannah's father, Reb Sigala. To their surprise, he too wanted to call off the wedding, but didn't know how. Things had gone from bad to worse in the Sigala household; Hannah had finally stopped crying, but she had also stopped eating, and Reb Sigala and his wife were beside themselves with worry. What if they forced this marriage on their only daughter? Would she just waste away?

After a few bewildered words and much hand-wringing, the three fathers decided they were out of their depth. They would have to ask the advice of my great-great-grandfather, Rabbi Shmul.

When they arrived at Grandpa's house he welcomed them in, and his wife, Helga, brought out the delicious tea and mandelbrot she always kept on hand for guests. Then one by one the fathers told their tale.

Reb Balta was the first to speak. "Rabbi, you know my son, Bessel, and you know, I'm sure, that he is engaged to be married to Reb Sigala's daughter, Hannah, and that Sarah the shadchen has already made all the arrangements. But now Hannah says she doesn't want to marry my son because he's so short. I ask you, Rabbi, is that his fault? Sure, he's short, but so what? He's a good boy, he doesn't drink, and he's admired by everyone, even the Russians. He's a hardworking young man, and he'll be an excellent husband to his wife and a good father to their children. Now Reb Drayzuch comes to me and says his son Ezek wants to marry Hannah instead. It's outrageous, Rabbi. Is there no way to make anyone happy in this ghetto anymore?"

Reb Sigala spoke next. "It is true, Rabbi, just as Reb Balta has said. We made all the arrangements with Sarah, and we thought everything was final. But my Hannah is not happy; she weeps constantly; she will not eat, she cannot sleep, and she insists that she cannot live the rest of her life with a man who barely reaches her bosom. It would be unheard of to break the engagement now. But how will my daughter ever be content in this marriage?"

Reb Drayzuch spoke last. "It is all true, Rabbi, just as my friends have said. But Rabbi, the marriage has not yet taken place; only the arrangements have been made. You know my son, Ezek, would make a good husband for any girl. He wants to marry Hannah very much—says he's 'in love' with her, and that she loves him as well. Rabbi, I know it's unusual, but there must be some way to call off this engagement. It will never end well, we can all see that, and if anyone can intervene, it is you. What shall we do?"

Rabbi Shmul sat stroking his beard, deep in contemplation. At last he sighed and looked up at each of the three distraught fathers. "My friends," he said slowly, "this is not an easy problem. The lifelong happiness of three families is at stake. It is a serious matter, and it is a problem the likes of which we have never seen in our ghetto before.

"Gentlemen, we must admit that times have

changed. In the past it was sufficient for us to make marriage arrangements for our children based on our own understanding of what would be a good alliance between families. But Reb Drayzuch has touched the heart of the matter by saying his son and Hannah are 'in love.' It is clear to me that our good intentions are no longer enough now that love has entered the picture.

"What is love? It is the need to belong to another, a desire to be joined forever, to be not just two individuals, but a unified couple, and to enjoy one life shared between two people.

"Of course, we must continue to help our children find satisfactory marriages; but in today's world we must also, whenever possible, take into account the feelings of our children themselves."

Rabbi Shmul addressed Reb Sigala. "Your Hannah is indeed a beautiful child, and one who is capable of much love. To force her into a marriage in which there is no love would be to condemn her to a life of emptiness. She is not yet seventeen years of age. Perhaps her marriage could wait another year or so."

He then turned to Reb Balta. "Bessel is a wonderful youth. True, he is not a tall man; but what he lacks in physical stature he more than makes up for with his skillful hands, his bright mind, and his good heart. Love and happiness are as important to him as to Hannah. I have no doubt that, given time, he could easily find a girl who could love him as much as he would love her, and for this reason, too, I think it is best to wait."

Finally he turned to Reb Drayzuch. "Ezek is surely a fine young man, and we must try to assure him a bright future. To marry now, in the face of a broken agreement, would only engender ill will among all our people, and it would almost guarantee that his marriage would not be happy—neither for him, for his wife, nor for their children. For his sake, too, I think this marriage should be postponed."

And so the marriage of Bessel and Hannah was put off. After a time it was forgotten, and eventually the wisdom of Rabbi Shmul's advice became apparent.

Within the year Bessel met Taifal, the daughter of Reb Gozonik, a lovely girl who was even a bit shorter than he. And after Sarah completed the new arrangements, Rabbi Shmul married them, to the delight of all.

Hannah's father arranged her marriage to Yamudik, the son of Rabbi Shonkeit of the village of Petuskiok. He was a tall youth, even taller than Hannah, and was loved by all who knew him, but especially by his wife-to-be.

As for Ezek, he emigrated to America, and before the year was out he wrote to his father that he had met the girl of his dreams in Chicago and that he intended to make her his wife. Ezek became a printer in the new land, and Reb Drayzuch was the proudest man in the entire ghetto when a year later he received a second letter telling him that he was now the grandfather of twin boys.

The Loner

ONE OF GRANDPA Shmul's closest friends was Father Pietr, the Russian Orthodox priest for the entire Orsha district. Over the years they not only became friends, but also came to consider each other colleagues, despite their different religions. And although they agreed not to debate religion, they often enjoyed discussing the affairs of the day over a glass of hot tea, and the rabbi and the father often helped each other solve the complex problems their parishioners brought them.

One day Father Pietr arrived at Rabbi Shmul's home obviously distressed. Helga invited him in and served tea and slices of her famous mandelbrot, which had always been one of the father's favorite treats. But as the two men sat down to the table, the priest neither ate nor drank as usual, nor did he speak. Instead he sat brooding, becoming more and more anxious as he debated with himself how to explain to his friend the problem that was plaguing him. Shmul was understanding and waited patiently until finally the priest, with a deep sigh, took a bite of mandelbrot and a sip of tea and began this woeful tale.

"In my congregation there is a young man of about twenty-four years," he said. "Of course, I cannot reveal his name, for reasons I'm sure you understand, Rabbi; but let us call him Shim. I have known this young man all his life; in fact, I had the pleasure of baptizing him into our faith shortly after he was born.

"From the very first, Shim seemed somehow different from other people. Even as a child he rarely established friendships, but spent most of his time alone. When other children were to be seen playing games together, Shim could be found off by himself somewhere; and when occasionally he did join in their games, it was only for a short time, as a guest, an outsider.

"Something seemed to be troubling little Shim, but I was never able to discover what it might be. As time passed he seemed to become more and more estranged, and I became increasingly concerned. I began to worry about him constantly, and I must admit that he was in my prayers more than most of our other congregants. But each time I found an opportunity to ask the boy what the matter was, I received the same short answer: 'I'm okay.'

"Nor were Shim's parents concerned about their son. They seemed not to notice that he was different from other children. When I cautiously broached the subject to them, they insisted that Shim was a bright and happy boy. He was the apple of their eyes—the more so as, despite his parents' efforts, they never conceived another child.

"But Shim's alienation seemed only to grow. Occasionally he sang in our choir—but only occasionally. One time I even asked my assistant to try to get him to join as a regular member, but he refused, although he had a very fine voice. And of course, Shim never invited others to join him in whatever he was doing; he seemed simply to prefer to do it alone. I suspect he never accepted invitations to the other children's parties, if he was ever invited at all. By the time he turned ten, Shim had earned a reputation as a loner, and other children began to avoid him.

"Years passed, and eventually Shim's classmates began to take an interest in girls—but not Shim. During choir practice the other boys would giggle and gossip in whispers about girls, but Shim stood silently until it was time to sing. I occasionally noticed that whenever a girl sat next to him at Mass, he would quickly move to another pew. And if a girl should speak to him, his face would blush crimson and he would abruptly walk off, leaving the girl looking amazed and wondering what she might have said to upset him. Even as Shim grew beyond puberty and became an adult, his interest in girls never seemed to develop.

"When he grew older, Shim got a job with the railroad, and he was often away from Orsha on business. I learned this when I noticed his absence at Mass. Despite his isolation—or perhaps because of it—he was a very observant Orthodox Christian and one of our most faithful worshipers. But then one Sunday I noticed he wasn't in the congregation, and when I didn't see him the following week, I asked his father if Shim was all right. 'You probably don't know,' the father answered, 'but Shim works for the railroad and is often away from home several days at a time. But don't worry. He's a good boy, and he assures us he goes to Mass wherever he is.'

"Finally things started to look brighter when it was announced that Shim was to be married to Marka, a beautiful girl from a very fine family. At last, I thought, the boy has come out of his shell; but what his father told me a few days later set me to worrying all over again. 'Last year I spoke to my son about marriage,' he said. 'This was not the first time I had raised the subject, but Shim had never responded more than to shrug it off and insist he wasn't interested. But this time, to my surprise, he became quite upset and pleaded with me to drop the subject and leave it alone. Yet I could not get it off my mind, and so I spoke with our marriage arranger, Bada. It was she who told me about Marka, and she seemed excited by the prospect of marrying her and Shim to one another. Marka's family was also agreeable, and my wife and I became enthusiastic. But when I spoke to my son, he resisted again and begged me to leave it alone. So I went back to Bada and asked her to speak to Shim herself. She promised to do so that very day. I don't know what she told him, but she must have changed his mind, for the next day he came to me to say he would agree to the marriage. My wife and I were thrilled and relieved, and we told Bada to go ahead and make the arrangements.'"

Father Pietr paused to sip his tea, but the dark look on his face told Shmul that the story wasn't over yet.

The priest continued, "I performed the marriage ceremony a month ago, and I prayed that all would be well. But it wasn't. Shim and Marka had been married only two weeks when Shim was called away by the railroad. Marka desperately missed her husband. She became despondent, and remained shut up in their house. But when Shim returned last week, the worst had happened: his young wife lay dead in her bed.

"It was a tragedy, and it was a mystery. The young woman was the image of robust health; there seemed to have been no foul play, for the house was still perfectly in order, and no mark could be found on her body. Nor was there a suicide note, nor any other evidence at all. The police report said that Marka had died of 'natural causes,' and estimated the time of death to have been about forty-eight hours before Shim discovered her body. It was assumed she had suffered a heart attack, but of course there was no autopsy."

The priest was by now sunk in his chair, his chin on his breast, and warm tears came from his eyes as his tea grew cold in his hands. "It was only yesterday, my friend, that I learned the true circumstances of that ill-fated marriage, and I have lived in a bewildered world since. Yesterday morning a man entered the confessional, and I immediately recognized poor Shim. He confessed to me that his marriage had never been consummated, though he insisted he had tried his very best. He loved his wife dearly, he claimed, and he was eager to begin a family with her. But when push came to shove— you'll pardon the expression, Rabbi—he simply felt no desire. He never had known desire, as I had suspected for many years; he was like a man who has no taste for music or literature but is forced to take part against his will.

"His wife, Shim confessed, would not leave him alone. At first she plied him with womanly ways, trying constantly to tempt him. But when this failed, she began crying and pleading for a normal marital life, driving him to distraction. When this too failed, she began to argue with him, to cajole, and to nag. How would they ever have children, she demanded, if he would not perform? How could she enjoy married life if he would not satisfy her? He insisted to her—and confessed to me—that it was not that he *would* not, but that he *could* not. But still she went on nagging and nagging, day and night, until he knew he must put a stop to it or he would go utterly mad.

"Now, as you know, my very dear friend, divorce

is not recognized by our church; only death may separate an Orthodox couple. There seemed to be no way out, and yet Shim was desperate that something be done—and quickly. And then he remembered something he had found on one of his railroad trips: a small bottle of rat poison left behind by some passenger. He had pocketed the bottle not knowing what he might do with it, but now an evil use occurred to him. Shim told me his mind revolted when he first thought of poisoning his wife, but as another week of nagging passed, his thoughts turned again and again to the little green bottle that seemed to offer a way out of his predicament.

"He devised a plan. It would be perfect. Before he set out on his next railroad assignment, he would slip the fine white powder from the bottle into the sugar that his wife added generously to her bedtime tea. When he returned, he would be a free man again. He could not be accused of his wife's murder, for he would not have been present. And in the future he would remain free. He would return to the life of a loner, the life he loved; and if his father or Bada pressed him to remarry, he would be adamant in refusing on account of his enduring grief over Marka. And so, two weeks ago, Shim carried out his plan.

"When Shim finished his confession he was weeping openly, and his sobs wrenched my own heart as I listened. 'Please, Father,' he implored, 'absolve me of my sin! I swear to you I will remain a good Christian, as I have always been, and I will repent my deed until the end of time!' I was overcome with pity for the man who had been pushed to such lengths despite his own simple desire to remain alone. Yet how can I grant absolution for so heinous a crime? And Rabbi, it is I who must decide. I cannot go to the authorities, for confession is a sacred rite, and the confidentiality of the confessional is sacrosanct. No, it is only G-d, and I, his servant, who may solve this problem. Rabbi, what shall I do?" And with that Father Pietr wept bitter tears of frustration.

Helga arose, refilled the glasses of tea, and brought out more mandelbrot to replace the few pieces the rabbi and the priest had eaten. Shmul sat deep in thought. Finally he spoke. "This young man, Shim, is truly an unusual character, and he was faced with what was for him a desperate situation. What he did was inexcusable, there is no doubt of that. But in a way it can be understood.

"First, we must recognize that Shim was an only child, and the burden of being an only child is heavy. All of the expectations of the family fall upon him. Shim's father wanted grandchildren, no doubt, as any proud father would; and Bada was the more anxious to arrange a marriage for Shim because he was the only marriageable member of his family.

"Second, we must acknowledge that Shim is different from others. He is a loner, but what of it? Left to his own wishes, he would have led a life that was, for him, normal and happy. But again he was subject to pressures other children never faced. Parents always want their children to be like all other children, except they want them to shine somehow and stand out from the crowd. This is a blessing for which most parents hope. But his father never understood, much less appreciated, what made Shim different; he only wanted his son to live an ordinary life like ordinary people. This, for Shim, was impossible.

"Third, we must admit that Shim knew that what he planned to do was wrong, and that he himself was horrified by it. This does not excuse the crime, but it is important nevertheless, for I do not think he would ever do such a thing again. No, his conscience will be plagued forever by guilt, and the sight of Marka lying dead in her bed will return again and again to disturb his dreams. He will suffer as few others have ever suffered, and his torment will be the greater precisely because of the desire to be alone that drove him to his sin and that now leaves him nowhere to turn. For Shim will never change. I have no doubt he will remain a loner as long as G-d grants him life. And thus his only solace can be in G-d himself.

"Father, I know it is both right and wrong, but the only way you can help this boy is to absolve him and welcome him back into your congregation. His religious devotion is deep, and his repentance is genuine. Perhaps with prayer he will gain some peace and be able to live his life as his nature seems to require."

Father Pietr left the Rabbi's house thoughtful, but he was relieved by the solution suggested by Rabbi Shmul. The next day he absolved poor Shim and welcomed him back with open arms—arms that did not cling. Two days after that, Shim received another railroad assignment. And without a word to anyone, he boarded the train and left Orsha station, never to return.

❧

Two years later, Father Pietr received a letter with an exotic-looking stamp from somewhere in Asia, a place neither he nor Rabbi Shmul had ever heard of. The letter was from Shim, and was very brief. He said only that he had joined an order of monks who had taken a vow of silence as penitence for the sins of the world, and that he was well. There was no further explanation, but Father Pietr and Rabbi Shmul knew they had been right about the young man. He would remain a penitent loner the rest of his days, trying to blot from his memory the unforgivable deed for which he atoned.

Am I Alive,
Or Am I Dead?

ONE GHETTO TRADITION of long standing was for the older men of the community to gather at the shul on Friday afternoons to make preparations for the shabbes. Despite their poverty, the ghettoites were grateful to G-d for permitting them to live another week, and they were anxious to express their love for him. The women of the ghetto would supply offerings of food, such as challas, pickled herring, and other delicacies, while the men would supply the wine used for special blessings and the schnapps they loved to drink while making ready for the day of prayer.

In the nearby village of Lubanklalik lived an old tailor, Reb Moisha ben Yitzhak. Despite the meager living he was able to earn with a needle and thread, Reb Moisha had grown extremely fat—he must have weighed nearly a hundred and fifty kilos. And despite the trials of his life—his wife and children had been killed by the Cossacks during one of their horrific nighttime raids—he was one of the happiest and most beloved men in the ghetto.

There was no shul in Lubanklalik, so most of the Jews of that shtetl came every week to worship at the shul in Orsha, and Reb Moisha always helped in the preparations. Early every Friday morning he would hitch up his old horse to a rickety wagon and drive the several kilometers to Orsha, where he would tether the horse in the grassy yard behind the shul. He made certain to arrive before sunset, not only because he wanted to help with the preparations, but because it was forbidden to ride on the shabbes. After the Friday night services, therefore, he would walk back to Lubanklalik in the dark, and early Saturday morning he would return to Orsha to spend the entire day in prayer. After sunset on Saturday he would drive the horse and wagon back home.

One particularly fine Friday Reb Moisha arose even earlier than usual, feeling strong and fit as he had not felt in decades. After a small breakfast he hitched up his horse and set out, and arrived at the Orsha shul just before noon. He got right to work with the other men on their preparations. First they sampled some of the schnapps Reb Sigala had obtained from an itinerant merchant, then they tasted some of Reb Balta's homemade wine. Then again they tried the schnapps, then the wine, and so on and so on. By mid-afternoon they were all a little drunk, but it was not until the sun rode low in the sky that they discovered Reb Moisha out behind the shul, face down in the grass.

It took three men to roll Reb Moisha over, and they poured cold water on him, slapped his face, and called his name. "Moisha! Moisha, wake up! Moisha! Speak to us!" But the old man lay still as a poached fish, and when they pulled back his eyelids they saw only the whites of his rolled-up eyes. Shames Drayzuch took hold of the old man's wrist and groped for a pulse, but he found none, and when he looked up at the bleary eyes around him, everyone knew that Reb Moisha was dead.

The men were stunned. They put the corks back in their preparations and pondered what to do. Only an hour or so of daylight remained, and it is forbidden to bury a corpse on the shabbes. Sunday would be the next opportunity to hold a funeral, but that was a long time away, and since Reb Moisha was so far from home, they had no idea what they would do with his body until then. So at last they decided to see if they couldn't get him in the ground before the sun set.

With no small effort a dozen men lifted Moisha's still form and laid it in his own wagon; then they harnessed his horse and drove him out to the cemetery. One of the men donated a shroud, which may never be omitted from an Orthodox burial. But a casket they would have to forgo; there was no time to have one built, and it would have been an expensive luxury, anyway. Many ghettoites were simply buried in their shrouds.

By the time they got to the cemetery the sun was rapidly nearing the horizon, and the men went right to work digging the grave. Years earlier a plot had been chosen for Moisha beside those of his wife and children, so they wasted no time surveying but dug right in.

They had only dug three feet or so when Reb Drayzuch looked up and said, "My brothers, we must stop our work. The sun is beginning to set; the shabbes is almost here." The others looked up and saw the reddened disk slipping slowly behind the trees that bordered a distant field, and they knew the shames was correct. Even if they did continue digging, it would be fully dark by the time they finished, and they would be unable to bury Moisha.

Regretfully, the men laid aside their spades and wondered what to do with the body. They didn't relish the idea of dragging him back to the shul, for it had taken a great effort to get him to the cemetery. They finally decided to leave him in the cemetery, and they promised him with teary eyes to return on Sunday after the shabbes and finish the task. Then they unhitched the horse and led it away, leaving their old friend in the wagon.

During the night Moisha ben Yitzhak awoke from his alcoholic stupor. He rose groggily to a sitting position, upsetting the wagon and dumping himself onto the ground right next to his own half-dug grave. Moisha just stared at the clods for a moment, then suddenly a thought formed through the fog in his brain and Reb Moisha cried out to the stars:

"Dear G-d—blessed be thy holy name—help me! Am I living, or am I dead? Oy, this can't be heaven, or my head wouldn't hurt so bad. But if this is Gehenna, why is it so freezing cold? If I am alive, what am I doing in the cemetery in the middle of the night? And if I am dead, why do I have to pee so bad?"

The Mikveh that Leaked

AMONG THE BUILDINGS to be found in the ghetto of Orsha, as in any Jewish community of Poland or Czarist Russia, was the mikveh, or ritual bathhouse. In Orsha, the mikveh was built in the basement of the shul and was fed directly by a deep spring that also supplied drinking water for the shul. But despite its location, the mikveh was not, as some Russians may have supposed, a Jewish baptismal font; baptism is not recognized by Judaism. It was, rather, a place for women to go to cleanse themselves of certain physical impurities unique to women, as Jewish law prescribes. Orthodox faith also requires a bride-to-be to immerse herself in the mikveh in order to wash away any past sins, real or imagined, so as to appear pure and sinless before her bridegroom. Also, again according to the law of Orthodox Jews, married women were required to visit the mikveh after each menstrual period and before resuming sexual relations with their husbands. But men are not permitted to enter the mikveh, except under special circumstances—as for example when repairs are needed—and then only with the expressed permission of the shames.

Cleanliness is one of the basic tenets of Judaism. It is mentioned in the Torah, and is practiced in many forms throughout Jewish life. But the mikveh is no ordinary bathtub. Its use goes back many centuries to the very early days of Judaism. It is mentioned in the scriptures, and was surely in use long before the destruction of the first temple in Jerusalem. Some authorities say that even new cooking vessels made by non-Jews should be immersed in the mikveh before being used, although such an occasion never arose in Orsha. In one tract of the Talmud it is said that a child born of a woman who has not ritually bathed in the mikveh should be considered a momser (bastard), although this opinion is not generally accepted. Maimonides wisely pointed out that the purpose of the mikveh was not to provide physical cleanliness, but rather the more essential spiritual cleanliness. Arhey Carmel, in the *New Standard Jewish Encyclopedia*, says that an Orthodox community may exist without a shul, for the people can pray in their homes; but such a community must have a mikveh, or its people cannot meet the requirements of Judaic law.

There is a well-known story about a group of Jews centuries ago who established themselves atop the stone mountain Masada in a futile attempt to escape the legions of Rome. Although they were beset with severe difficulties in scratching a living from the mountain's rocky soil and building a habitable community on its steep slopes, the first thing they did upon arrival was build a mikveh, so that their women could follow the rituals of Orthodoxy.

There are also recognized standards for building a mikveh, some of which run to considerable detail. These include such considerations as the maximum and minimum amount of water needed to achieve a proper cleansing of the spirit, materials of which the mikveh may be built, and methods of filling, cleaning, and emptying the mikveh. It is further stipulated that any leak in the mikveh shall render it unclean. These rules have been set down many times throughout history, with all the contradictions and differences of opinion one might expect from generations of scholarly argument.

Now, it appeared one day that the mikveh at the Orsha shul had developed a leak. Elka-Chana was the first to notice that the level of the water was slowly but perceptibly declining day by day, and she reported her finding to Reb Drayzuch, the shames of the shul. As soon as Reb Drayzuch determined that the mikveh was unoccupied, he went to examine it and found that there was indeed a leak, so he hung out a small sign saying the the mikveh was closed for repairs and went to summon Reb Bessel, the plumber who always took care of such things at the shul.

At about the same time, Shmulke-Levika had just completed her menstrual period and, unaware that the mikveh was under repair, she was headed for the shul to bathe, for she was anxious to resume normal life with her husband. She entered without noticing the small sign Shames Drayzuch had posted, and only wondered for a moment why she was the only woman there. She did notice that the water was cooler than usual and that it wasn't as deep as usual, but she paused only long enough to make a mental note to scold the shames for neglecting his duty, then went about her business. She sank down in the water, relaxed, and was just beginning to enjoy herself when, to her horror, the door creaked open and in walked Bessel.

"Gevalt!" she shouted, loud enough to be heard in the next village. Not expecting male company, she had not even prepared a towel to cover her nakedness, and she later claimed that Bessel stared and stared—although he vehemently denied this accusation.

Reb Bessel departed in a big hurry, and that should have ended the episode. Would have ended it, too, had not Shmulke been the yenta she was; for to permit so good a story to die untold was anathema to her. For days thereafter the story was ever on her lips. She recounted it, in all its original detail and more, to anyone who would listen, adding artfully to it with each recounting until Bessel became a "peeping Tom" and she his "helpless victim."

The story spread from mouth to mouth, as do all good stories in all small towns, and as it did its already rich detail grew more and more lurid. By the time it reached the ears of my great-great-grandfather Shmul it had been exaggerated out of all proportion, and the poor rabbi was horrified to learn that Shmulke-Levika had been raped in the mikveh! Oy! Such a thing was unheard of in the ghetto!

Grandpa Shmul knew, of course, that in the foot-race of gossip a good story will lap the truth every time, and so he summoned Reb Bessel to the shul to tell him what had really happened. Reb Bessel explained that Shames Drayzuch had called him to repair the leaking mikveh, and pointed out that the shames had posted a sign saying that the mikveh was temporarily closed. Indeed, upon inspection Shmul verified that the sign was still in place, although it was small, like almost everything Reb Drayzuch did. But Reb Bessel denied any assault, physical or visual, upon Shmulke-Levika. "The shames said it was okay for me to enter, but as soon as I noticed there was somebody in there, I turned right around and ran. I tried to find the shames, but he had left the shul. Rabbi, I didn't even know who the woman in the mikveh was; I only learned her name when I heard the gossip from my wife that I had raped her!"

Grandpa immediately realized that Bessel's story

was the truth, paltry though it was in comparison to the spectacular rumor that had outrun it. He called Shames Drayzuch, Shmulke-Levika and her husband Chaim, and Bessel's wife Taifal to come to the shul to put an end to the awful rumor of rape. One by one they aired the facts of the case and winnowed out the fiction; and even though Shmulke refused to admit that she had embroidered the story like a formal ball gown, the truth finally caught up with and overtook the rumor. Reb Bessel returned home exonerated.

Thus, in the mikveh of Orsha as elsewhere, the slow and steady turtle of truth won the race against the rabid rabbit of rumor.

The Shabbes Dinner Was Late

ONE OF THE inviolable rules of Orthodox Judaism is that there may be no cooking on the shabbes; nor may there be any lighting of fires, which in rural Russia of the nineteenth century amounted to the same thing. This is because cooking is a form of work, as any housewife will attest, and all work is proscribed on the shabbes. In those days the biggest meal of the day, a hot dinner, was usually served at noon, while the evening supper was a light repast, little more than a snack. This is still the custom in many parts of Europe today. But on the shabbes, although the women knew their

48

husbands preferred a hot dinner when they came home from the shul at noon, they would not think of defying the law by lighting a cooking fire. Therefore they had to either serve cold leftovers, or devise some other strategy for preparing a hot meal. Eventually this problem was solved in a simple way that quickly became very popular.

In Orsha, as elsewhere, it was the custom of the two Jewish bakeries to bake enough challas every Friday morning for all the families in the ghetto, plus a few extras for the several neighboring Russians who came to the ghetto to buy these delicious breads. The challa, a type of egg bread, is the special contribution of Jewry to the world of baking. It is sometimes round, but usually long and braided; it is always made of the very best ingredients, sometimes with raisins added, and its cake-like morsels melt in the mouth. Challas grace every Jewish table on Friday nights, and are also served at most holiday dinners. It is the custom never to slice the challa before the blessing has been recited, and in some Orthodox homes the challa is broken rather than sliced. It is said that some Jewish homes have two challas on the table, in memory of the days during which the Jews wandered in the desert; but in the ghetto of Orsha the poor families were happy to have just one.

The bakers' work of preparing challas began very early Friday morning so that it would be finished not later than three o'clock in the afternoon, before the shabbes began at sundown. The bakeries had huge brick ovens, and on Fridays their fires were lit earlier than on other days. When the bricks were sufficiently heated, the fires would be allowed to die out, and the hot bricks baked the bread. When the loaves developed crisp, shining crusts and their tempting aroma filled the bakery and wafted out to the street, they were removed with large wooden paddles.

But the bricks in the ovens remained hot for many hours more, even until the middle of the following day. And that was what allowed the Jewish families of the ghetto to serve hot meals on the shabbes without lighting a fire.

On Fridays, the women of the ghetto began preparing a cholent, a one-pot meal for the shabbes. Into a large, deep, cast-iron pot they carefully placed a small ceramic dish, and in this they set noodles, raisins and other fruit, sugar, and cinnamon, all of which they then covered with a well-beaten egg. This would become a delicious kugel pudding, a dessert fit for G-d's own angels. Around the kugel dish the women then arranged peeled potatoes, vegetables, and cut-up strips of meat—usually brisket or flanken. Then they covered the pot and carefully placed the potato peelings atop it for insulation, and finally they wrapped the whole thing in old newspaper and tied it securely with string. Then one of the children, usually the eldest, took the prepared cholent to the bakery to be cooked by the hot bricks of the ovens.

The bakers received nearly identical pots from almost every family in the ghetto, so they had to devise a way to keep them from becoming mixed up. For each pot the baker wrote two identical numbers on a piece of paper, which he tore in half; one half was fixed securely to the pot, and the other half was given to the child to whom the pot belonged. In return, the child would give the baker the few coins the family had provided to pay for the baking. The following day the children returned to the bakery, where the bakers pulled the completely baked and still-hot cholents from the oven with their long wooden paddles and called out the numbers affixed to them. The slips of paper were scorched by the heat of the oven, but they never burned, because there was no fire. The child with the matching number claimed his pot of cholent and returned home with a savory stew, complete with a delicious kugel for dessert, hot and ready to eat—and all without so much as lighting a match.

Reb Nachem ben Ary was the owner of the larger of the two bakeries in the Orsha ghetto, and he had hired a Russian lad of subnormal intelligence, Hofik, to help him. Hofik's duties were to fill the huge ovens with wood before dawn each morning, to light the fires to heat the bricks, to keep the bakery clean, and occasionally to wrap bread for the customers. But Nachem himself prepared the numbers for the shabbes cholents, for he knew that even the slightest error would surely lead to an argument.

One Friday, however, Nachem was called away on an urgent task. As he hastily hung up his apron he asked Hofik, "Have you seen how I write out the numbers for the cholent, two on each slip of paper?"

"Sure," answered the willing, if not too bright, lad. "Two on each slip of paper."

"Good," said Nachem. "Today the children will deliver their pots of cholent, and I want you to be very careful in numbering them."

"I will, boss, don't you worry," Hofik assured him, and Nachem dashed off on his errand. It never occurred to him that he should have told Hofik to write the same number twice on each slip of paper.

At noon that day the children began to arrive with their stew pots, just as Nachem had said, and Hofik dutifully began to write the numbers on little slips of paper, two numbers on each. On the first he carefully wrote a 1 and a 2. On the second he wrote 3 and 4. Then he neatly tore the slips of paper in two, exactly as he had seen his boss do, affixing the odd numbers to the pots and giving the even numbers to the children. Soon the oven was full of odd-numbered pots, and Hofik closed the shop and went home proud of having fulfilled his responsibility so well.

The next morning Reb Nachem returned to the bakery just as the children arrived to pick up their cholents. He picked up his wooden paddle and pulled out the first pot and called out "Number one!" But nobody came forward to claim it. This had never happened before, and Nachem was perplexed; but he figured the child must be late, so he put the pot back into the oven and drew out the next one. "Number three!" he called. Again, no claimant. This was indeed irregular, he thought;

and what had happened to number two? But he couldn't think with the clamor of the children all around him, so he replaced the pot and drew out the next. "Number five!" Still no taker.

Now Nachem knew something was wrong. He pulled Hofik aside. "Did you number the pots like I told you? And did you put half of the slip on the pot and give the other half to the child?" Hofik assured him he had. So Nachem returned to the oven and pulled out another pot, but when he saw its number, seven, something clicked.

"What number have you got?" he asked the nearest child. It was number two. "Let's see yours," he asked another. There was number four! And all around him were children with slips of paper numbered six, eight, ten, twelve, and so on.

With a sinking feeling, Nachem realized what had happened. But in the same instant he realized that Hofik's madness must have a method to it. The pot numbered one must belong to child number two; pot three must belong to child four; and so on. So, by adding one to the number of each pot, he finally succeeded in reuniting each child with his family's dinner. And although the process took some time, the food was still kept warm by the hot oven bricks when the last child received his pot.

That's how the entire ghetto of Orsha had a late dinner one shabbes many years ago. Oh well, thought Reb Nachem as he wearily closed his shop that evening. Maybe the meal will taste better for the wait!

Which Baby Is He?

THINGS WERE QUIET in the ghetto. Somehow almost a month had passed without tsouris—no deaths, no disputes, no moral quagmires to be waded—and now Rabbi Shmul sat by the fire trying in vain to think of something that would make an interesting sermon for the next shabbes. Then came a knock on the door, arousing him to enter again the real world. Helga, the rebbitsin, went to answer the door and immediately recognized Mr. Zivorka, the Polish-born Russian who owned and edited the small Orsha newspaper. The rabbi and the editor had not seen each other since more than a year ago, when they met by chance on the streets of Orsha. They had stopped for a schnapps and had a

pleasant visit, reminiscing about the days when
young Shmul earned money for his rabbinical studies by working for the newspaper as a "gofer," doing
whatever odd jobs the editor needed done in the offices and in the press room. He also traveled
weekly to Smolensk, the nearest big city, to fetch
the national and world news from Zivorka's cousin,
who edited the Smolensk *Gazette*. Those had been
exciting times for the lad, and he frequently came
back to Orsha with some strange story he had
heard along the way. At their last meeting the
rabbi and the editor had passed the afternoon
laughing and enjoying again those odd tales.

But it was a rare occasion that brought the editor to the ghetto, and Rabbi Shmul suspected he
had come to ask a favor. He was right.

"Rabbi," Zivorka greeted him formally instead of
by his first name as he used to do, but he still
spoke in Polish, as he always had. "I hate to impose
on you, but you're the only person I know who can
help. My gofer is ill, and I need someone to go to
Smolensk today or tomorrow to pick up the news.
Now that you're a rabbi, I wouldn't ask you to go
third-class like you used to do, but I'd be happy to
supply a first-class ticket if you can find the time to
help me. I'd be grateful forever if you would make
just this one more trip."

The editor didn't mention any compensation, but
Shmul still felt indebted to him for having given
him a job when he needed it. "Certainly, Mr.
Zivorka," he replied. "I'd be happy to help you. But
a first-class ticket isn't necessary; rabbis can ride

third-class just as well as anyone else. As a matter of fact, I think I would enjoy the trip. I haven't been out of Orsha in years, and I'd love to see your cousin again. And who knows," he added with a sly grin, "I might even meet some interesting people along the way."

And so it was that the next day Shmul again found himself sitting on a hard wooden bench in a third-class compartment on the train to Smolensk. Even before the train left the station he was lost in reverie, dreaming of the adventurous days of his youth. But his daydream was broken when the door opened and a man and his wife entered and asked politely if they might share the compartment with him. Each carried a small baby wrapped in a colorful blanket, and as they seated themselves Shmul stole a closer look and saw that the babies looked exactly alike. They must be twins, he thought.

The man introduced himself as Borenk Brevenkifa and the twins as Erek and Berek. Shmul noticed that he didn't introduce his wife. She seemed a meek woman, deferring to her husband with an inclined head and averted eyes, yet she looked very proud of her sons as they were introduced. But in the male-dominated world of nineteenth-century Russia, the omission seemed unimportant. "This one is Erek," the man said, pointing, "and that one is Berek. I'll bet you can't tell them apart. My wife can, but I couldn't do it to save me until I came up with a special scheme, which works very well. You see, I cut Erek's hair every week or two, but I never cut Berek's, and that's how I tell them apart. The baby with long hair is Berek, and the one with short hair is Erek."

What a very odd way to identify one's own children, thought Shmul. But the man explained, "Before I thought up that trick the boys always confused me. They're quite identical otherwise, as you can see, so there's no telling them apart by looks. When they cry, which they do often, their voices are identical, so that doesn't help; both of them always have wet diapers, so that doesn't help either; and they both nurse like hungry young lions. They're exactly the same in every way, so I had to figure out some way to mark them, as it were."

With that the man sat back and beamed proudly, although Shmul couldn't tell whether it was pride of his twins or of his own invention. Then he saw that the man's right arm was missing, the empty sleeve pinned to his shoulder. The man noticed Shmul's gaze, but he didn't seem at all shy about it.

"Missing a wing, I am," he said loudly as he moved his shoulder back and forth, causing the empty sleeve to wave in the air. "Lost it in the army in aught-seven. We were on war games in the woods; our unit was looking for a group of cavalry who were playing the enemy, and the captain sent six of us forward into the forest on recon. We couldn't find them cavalrymen anywhere, so we made camp for the night. We stacked our guns and ammunition in a pile, pitched our tents, and built a fire. We thought we had built the fire far enough from the ammo, but it was a bad mistake. Sometime during the middle of the night a spark must have drifted from the fire, and the whole camp blew sky high. Everyone else was killed, but I was lucky; I was the furthest from the fire, but still it blew my arm clean off, and I was bleeding like a stuck pig. Fortunately the blast brought help quickly. The field surgeon had to remove what was left of the stump, and I was discharged and sent home. They told me I'd get a pension, but...." The man shrugged his shoulders and rolled his eyes.

"Mr. Shmul, do you know how hard it is to find work with no right arm? Nobody will hire me, though G-d knows I've tried, and now we're reduced to living on charity from my wife's father. It's even harder now with Erek and Berek to take care of, and they do keep us busy. At least we have our family."

Shmul thought how foolish it was for the army to send out troops who didn't even know enough to keep their ammunition away from their campfire, and he felt sorry for the poor pensioner who would probably never see a kopek of his pension. Still, the man seemed to accept his fate, and he certainly maintained a creative outlook on life, as demonstrated by his imaginative way of distinguishing between his sons.

As the train pulled into Smolensk, the mother dressed each twin in a very pretty cap that she had crocheted herself. The caps completely covered the babies' heads, hiding their hair and making them indistinguishable once again. As Shmul and the couple alit from the carriage, the rabbi offered his help, and the man handed him one of the babies. Was it Erek? Or was it Berek? Shmul had lost track, and now that their heads were covered, there really was no way to tell!

Shmul went on to the *Gazette* offices, where he picked up the news and lunched with the editor, who was surprised and happy to see him again. Then Rabbi Shmul took the afternoon train back to Orsha.

"Well," said Mr. Zivorka, "how was the trip?"

"It was absolutely delightful," said Shmul, "and I met the most interesting family on the train…" and he proceeded to tell the editor about Erek and Berek and their distinctive hairstyles.

"You know," said the editor after he had listened to the tale, "it reminds me of an old saying I once heard: 'When hair grows upon the face, the boy has grown to a man.' But in this case I would say 'When hair grows upon the head, it must be Berek!'"

Who Stole the Afikomen?

As THE PESACH holiday approached, Shames Drayzuch had an idea, and he could hardly wait to tell the rabbi.

This was not unusual. As poor as the ghetto was in other commodities, it was a swank neighborhood for ideas. Hardly a week passed during which one of the ghettoites didn't hatch some scheme and come running breathlessly to reveal his inspiration to the rabbi in all its glorious detail. Shames Drayzuch was perhaps the most inventive of all. Unfortunately, few of these wild and vivid ideas were very practical—not even the few that made sense—and it was a challenge for my great-great-grandfather to find inoffensive words to tell their inventors that their ideas were flawed, unworkable, or just plain meshugge.

But here was the shames again, all fired up over something. "Rabbi," he began, "I've had the most wonderful idea!" Here it comes, thought Shmul. "You know, Rabbi, there are many people in our ghetto who have no family with whom to celebrate the Pesach seder. Widows, widowers, old couples whose children have moved away—come Pesach they are alone. So I thought, why not have a community seder at the shul? We could move back some of the benches to make room, and I could set out the tables and chairs from the storeroom; the back room with the water trough will serve as a kitchen, and we'll get the women to prepare the food and the men to help decorate and move furniture. I'll conduct the ceremonies and we'll have a huge big seder for everyone, right in our temple. Rabbi, it would be a real mitzvah."

To most of the ghettoites the shul was simply a shul, but to the shames it was always "our temple." And, thought Shmul, G-d only knows how much junk he's got stashed in the storeroom. But here, perhaps, was an idea worth considering. It was true that there were many lonely elderly people in the ghetto, and it must be hard for them indeed, especially during this holiday. There had never been a seder in the shul before, but…well, why not?

One problem occurred to Rabbi Shmul immediately. "What about the four kashas? These questions are an important part of the ceremony, and they should be asked by a child. But if we have such a seder, it will be attended by old people. So who will ask the kashas?"

But the shames had anticipated his question. "Don't worry, Rabbi, I've thought of everything. My wife has some cousins who live in Rachikov, and they have a young son. I'll invite them, and he can ask the kashas."

It seemed like a good solution, indeed. Rachikov was a very small shtetl several kilometers away that didn't have a shul, nor even a rabbi. Although travel by horse and wagon was arduous and no one enjoyed it much, they just might do it for the chance to attend a real Pesach seder with their family.

"Well," said the rabbi, "you seem to have thought this through very well, and it just might work. Let's try it. I think it could be a very great mitzvah for our lonely ghettoites."

My great-great-grandfather announced the idea to the congregation at the shul the next Friday evening, and though it was greeted with warm enthusiasm at first, after the service there was much skepticism and the usual quibbling over the details. Who would do the cooking—would one woman make all the matzo balls, or would everyone contribute her own favorite recipe? Would the menu be the traditional one, with soup, gefilte fish, and all, or would it have to be simplified? Would the food and the wine still be kosher after being carried all the way to the shul? Would the soup get cold? And, most importantly, who would be in charge of making sure all these details were worked out? But despite these concerns, everyone felt that a community seder would be a good way to bring people together, and in the end they agreed that if Shames Drayzuch could work out the details, the seder would be held.

The shames and his wife launched into the preparations immediately. They drew up a menu and recruited several women to help cook, serve, and clean up. Mrs. Drayzuch contacted her cousins, who promised they would come; and the shames got several ghetto men to volunteer to haul the furniture from the storeroom and clean it and repair it for the occasion. Spirits ran high throughout the ghetto. For all anyone knew, this might be the very first community seder in the history of the world, and it seemed like a better idea the closer it came to becoming a reality.

Came the month of Nisan and the eve of the seder, and all was ready. Rabbi Shmul went to the shul that morning and was overwhelmed by what he saw. The benches had been pushed back—except, of course, those along the eastern wall—and tables had been set out and spread with starched white linens and set with mismatched silverware and glasses donated by various households. The lectern had been moved aside and covered with oil-cloth to receive the dirty dishes. The Shames's wife had even brought fresh flowers, and extra candles to light up the dark corners of the room, and the shul looked bright and joyful as it never had before.

As soon as the sun set, the guests began to arrive, and they kept on arriving until the shul was bursting at the seams. Neither the shames nor the rabbi had imagined there were so many lonely people in the ghetto, but they were all the more glad they had decided to hold this celebration for them. Reb Drayzuch was seated at the head of the table to conduct the ceremony, and he beamed as brightly as the shul itself. To his right was seated the rabbi, ready to assist with the seder rituals and prepared to settle the arguments that would surely arise over every possible subject, from the order of the seder, to the correct wording of the Haggadah stories, to whether or not there was enough matzo for everyone. And all around the table were the happy faces of people who were no longer lonely.

Shames Drayzuch and Rabbi Shmul performed their offices well, and despite the inevitable quibbling, the seder progressed very smoothly. In fact, it got smoother as it went along and the celebrants drank first one, then two, then three cups of wine, and before long the whole affair was very well lubricated indeed.

Then it came time for one of the climaxes of the ceremony, in which the shames breaks a piece of matzo in two, one of which becomes the afikomen. Then as now, this was the children's favorite part of the seder, and it was traditional for them to "steal" the afikomen and hold it for a ransom of candy or coins, for the seder could not be concluded until the final blessing was made over the afikomen. Therefore, after Shames Drayzuch had broken the matzo and blessed it, he carefully hid the afikomen under the oilcloth on the lectern, as there was only one child in the room, his wife's nephew, and he was seated at the far end of the table.

Now, one of the women helping out at this seder was Shmulke-Levika, the yenta. Although she was primarily known for her loose tongue, she was equally notable for her tight housekeeping. The saying "cleanliness is next to godliness" may even have been invented by her. (In fact, almost everything she ever said was an invention.) When her husband smoked cigars, she emptied the ashtray at least twice during the smoke, for she couldn't bear to leave the ashes until the whole cigar was finished. Likewise, when she served a meal she cleared away each dish as it was emptied, and sometimes even before, for she couldn't stand to see dirty dishes remain on the table for even one minute.

So although there was only one child who might have stolen the afikomen, nevertheless it disappeared from under the oilcloth almost as soon as the shames had brushed the crumbs from his fingers. As Shmulke-Levika cleared the dishes from the lectern she didn't even notice the piece of matzo under the cloth; she hadn't seen the shames put it there, and she didn't know it was the afikomen. She scooped it up with the dirty dishes, and into the trash it went.

The seder continued without anyone noticing that the afikomen was missing. At the appointed time, the people opened the door to admit the invisible Elijah, and in the spirit of the event (augmented by the spirit of the wine), people said they felt his very presence. Then it came time to give the final blessing over the afikomen, and the shames reached under the oilcloth to retrieve it; only then did he notice it was gone.

All eyes immediately turned to Mrs. Drayzuch's nephew. He hadn't moved from his seat, but they frisked him anyway. Of course he didn't have the afikomen. Where could it be? In an instant the whole shul was in turmoil as people searched under tables and turned the place upside down.

Then Shmulke-Levika, who had been out back washing up, came in and found everyone on their hands and knees searching for the afikomen. "What on earth is going on here?" she asked the shames.

"The afikomen—it's disappeared! I hid it right here on the lectern, under the cloth, but now it's gone and we can't find it anywhere!"

"Oy, veh!" cried Shmulke-Levika. "Reb Drayzuch, you know the lectern is for the dirty dishes and table scraps. I must have cleared the afikomen away! Who ever heard of hiding the afikomen under the dirty dishes?" And to herself she added, "Such a shlemiel!"

Shmulke-Levika went back to the kitchen, and to everyone's infinite relief she returned a moment later with half a piece of matzo. But when the shames placed it next to the piece from which he had broken the afikomen, it was obvious that the ends didn't match.

"Wait a minute, Shmulke-Levika," he said. "This isn't the afikomen."

"What's the difference—matzo is matzo," she replied, adding again under her breath, "Such a shlemiel." But the shames insisted that only the real afikomen would do, and so she went back to the kitchen and brought out another half-piece of matzo. When it didn't fit, she returned for still another, and it was not until the fourth try that the real afikomen was found.

At last the shames gave the final blessing and distributed pieces of the afikomen to all, and the seder concluded with the drinking of the fourth cup of wine—which nobody really needed—and a rousing and off-key singing of the ghettoites' favorite Pesach song, "An Only Kid." They sang so loudly it seemed they were trying to reach the ears of G-d in heaven. The final dispute of the evening was over what to do with the cup of wine that had been set out for Elijah—nobody wanted to throw it out, for wine was expensive; but would it be proper to pour it back into the bottle? Rabbi Shmul wisely pointed out that the wandering prophet would surely not begrudge the poor ghettoites saving the unused wine for the following night's seder, and everyone applauded his decision as the wine was poured back.

So ended the world's first community seder, but its reputation lived on. In fact, its reputation continued to grow: even many years later, Shmulke-Levika could still be heard telling all who would listen about that shlemiel of a shames who had almost ruined the Pesach seder by getting drunk and losing the afikomen—and where had he hidden it? According to her later versions of the story, he'd hidden it inside the scrolls of the Torah!

The Inheritance

IT ALL HAPPENED because Shmulke-Levika, the gossiping yenta of Orsha, was on the train to Smolensk to attend her nephew Itzik's wedding. If she hadn't gone, there would be no story; but of course she went, even though she didn't like to travel, because it was her only nephew, an orphan whom she had raised as her son.

Itzik's parents, Shmulke-Levika's sister and brother-in-law, had been killed in a ghetto fire when their son was only an infant. Lightning struck their house during an electrical storm, and since ghetto houses were built of wood and the ghetto fire department was a volunteer bucket brigade, almost the entire neighborhood burned. Itzik was carried out of the blaze by a neighbor, and was only slightly burned. But when the neighbor returned to rescue the parents, it was too late. The house had become a raging inferno, puffing clouds of dense smoke. When finally the rain, aided by the somewhat feeble efforts of the bucket brigade, quenched the flames, only the charred remains of the parents were found.

Itzik was raised by his Aunt Shmulke-Levika and her husband, Chaim ben Yussel, and they became his devoted parents. The couple had no children of their own, and all their love was heaped upon the orphaned boy. Itzik proved to be a very intelligent lad, and when he was old enough, Chaim insisted that he be sent to cheder in Smolensk to prepare for his bar mitzvah. The school there was conducted by Rabbi Slovkovskik, a leader among rabbis in the region because of his genius at molding bright youngsters into educated and understanding Jewish adults. It took all the family's resources to send Itzik to Smolensk, but the boy showed such promise that they knew it would be worthwhile.

And it was. Shortly after Itzik began his studies, Rabbi Slovkovskik told Chaim and Shmulke-Levika that he was the brightest of all his pupils. And when Itzik neared the end of the curriculum, the rabbi urged that he stay on and study for the rabbinate.

Shmulke and Chaim were proud of their adopted son, but the family had other plans: Itzik was to be apprenticed to a tailor, Reb Fissel, in the ghetto of

Smolensk. They apologized to the rabbi, explaining that it was beyond their means to support Itzik for the years rabbinical study would require; in fact, they needed Itzik to help support the family as soon as possible. Itzik agreed with them, they insisted; he didn't want to become a rabbi, but preferred to have a trade and be his own boss.

So Itzik went to work for Reb Fissel, and again he excelled at his work. He remained with the tailor for two years and learned everything Reb Fissel knew about pressing, sewing, cutting patterns, and selecting and buying fabrics; and at the end of the boy's apprenticeship, Reb Fissel begged him to remain and become a partner in his business. Itzik's adoptive parents were reluctant when they learned the boy would have to remain in Smolensk, but he assured them that he would be able to help them even more as a partner in the business, and they finally relented.

In the spring in which Itzik turned nineteen, he met Rivka, the daughter of Reb Zitzo and his wife, Purala. Reb Zitzo owned the largest butcher shop in the ghetto of Smolensk, and was reputed to sell the very best brisket, flanken, and lamb chops in the entire city. Indeed, many town Russians came to the ghetto to buy Reb Zitzo's special cuts of meat, and the butcher became one of the few truly wealthy people in the ghetto. Itzik had met Reb Zitzo's daughter, Rivka, in the butcher shop one afternoon, and the couple were smitten as soon as their eyes met. It was love at first sight. In the next few weeks Rivka had her dresses altered and

re-altered at the tailor shop, and Itzik bought
Zitzo's brisket and flanken like there would be none
tomorrow. Before long the couple decided they
wanted to marry.

Itzik asked his uncle Chaim to come to Smolensk
and talk to Reb Zitzo about the possibility of his
marrying Rivka. Reb Chaim came happily, anxious
for Itzik to be wed, and the two men quickly agreed
to the match. Reb Zitzo contacted Raizel-Milov, the
shadchen of Smolensk, and asked her to arrange
the details. Although she was a bit put off because
she had not chosen the bride and groom herself as
she usually did, she agreed to make arrangements
for the wedding of Itzik and Rivka—for her usual
fee, of course—and a date was set.

And so it was that Chaim and Shmulke-Levika
found themselves in the third-class compartment of
the train from Orsha to Smolensk, en route to the
wedding of their nephew. In the compartment they
met a Christian couple who informed them they
were going all the way to Moscow, where they lived.
They had been visiting their son and his wife in a
village named Karalenkov, well beyond Orsha, and
had seen their first grandchild born, and they were
now returning, proud and happy grandparents.

This opening to conversation was all Shmulke-
Levika needed to start up the rumor mill that was
her tongue. She told them all the latest news from
Orsha—who was marrying whom, who had lost a
job, who was ill or well—embellishing the stories as

only she could have done. Never mind that the couple had never heard of Orsha, were not Jews, and couldn't possibly care about the petty affairs of a miserable little ghetto; never mind that they couldn't understand the spicy Yiddish expressions that peppered her speech; once Shmulke got started, there was no stopping her.

But one story in particular piqued the man's interest. "In Orsha we have a man who had an old spinster aunt he almost never saw," Shmulke-Levika told him. "She lived in Divornekov, a little village up north somewhere—do you know it?" As usual, she did not wait for a reply, but continued without missing a beat. "Anyway, this aunt up and died, and you'll never believe it, she left him all her money! He hardly knew her, even—couldn't even remember her name until he got the money—and they say it was plenty, too, I can tell you that. Anyway, you'll never believe what that shlemiel did next. He started putting on airs, getting all uppity and full of himself just because he was rich. Suddenly we ghetto people weren't good enough for him, no sir, and he wouldn't even talk to some of us. And he kept every single kopek for himself— would you believe it? He never gave to the poor, though the Lord knows we've got plenty of poor in Orsha. But not a kopek would he give, the teivel. He thinks he knows better than anyone, and he expects everyone to do just what he says! Such a shlemiel!

"Only one thing would he part with," Shmulke continued. She paused and looked around the compartment suspiciously, then drew from the folds of her dress a little package neatly wrapped in colorful cloth. "This is it—the aunt's priceless heirloom brooch!" She held out the package for the man and woman to see, but as soon as they made to touch it, she snatched it away and stuffed it back inside her dress. "I'm taking it as a wedding present for my nephew's wife in Smolensk, and I don't want to unwrap it; but I can tell you it is such a brooch! Solid silver, and with stones all around it—oy, it weighs a ton, with all those jewels. Well, it's not something I would wear, personally, but she'll like it, I'm sure. And I paid a tidy little sum to get it out of the hands of that shmendrick, I can tell you that! How much? Well, not nearly what it was worth! He's not very bright, that shlemiel."

"What is the name of this, er, gentleman?" asked the Russian man.

"Reb Shmolskit is his name. We call him Shmendrick, but all he is is a good-for-nothing shlemiel," Shmulke answered.

The Russian man raised a bushy eyebrow as he tried to remember the name and the epithet. For he was, as it happened, a supervisor in the czar's tax department, and Shmulke-Levika's story had roused his professional curiosity. When he arrived back at his Moscow office, he checked the ledger for the town of Orsha to see if this person had paid the inheritance tax. First he looked for a Mr. Shmendrick, but found nothing. Then he looked for Shmolskit, and there he was: Shmolskit, a resident of the Orsha ghetto. A damn Jew! He might have known. Of course, no inheritance tax had been paid. For that matter, no one in the ghetto had paid an inheritance tax in over ten years. It did look irregular.

The tax agent decided to take matters into his own hands. He could simply go to Orsha, visit the ghetto, collect the tax and beat the daylights out of this Mr. Shlemiel, or Shlemolski, or whatever the hell his name was. But that would be too easy. He wanted to make an real example of this Jew, one that the ghettoites would never forget, and so he devised a plan.

A few days later a peasant entered the Orsha ghetto saying he was from Siberia, where, he claimed, the reputation of the rabbi of Orsha was well known and respected. There was no rabbi in his village, and so his people had sent him as a representative to meet with this erudite rabbi, he said, and to learn from his wisdom.

But something about the man didn't seem right. For one thing, he didn't look Jewish; but he said he was from Siberia, and after all, who knew what a Siberian Jew looked like? Nor did he speak Yiddish, but only Russian, for which he apologized saying that there was no Jewish education to be had in his village—no cheder, no shul, nothing. He had relocated to that cold land of tundra with his parents, who were both Jews, he said, to seek their fortune, and he had been so deprived in that wasteland that he didn't even know the prayers. Indeed, he said, that was precisely why he had come to Orsha.

Nevertheless, the ghettoites were sympathetic, and they were sufficiently flattered not to doubt that the reputation of their own Rabbi Shmul had spread to the far reaches of the country. Reb Gashonik, the tinker, even agreed to take the stranger into his home and told him he might stay there as long as his studies with Rabbi Shmul continued.

The next day the stranger went to see the rabbi. He told him his sad story, and inquired about life in a ghetto in Russia in the time of the czars. By and by he had a chance to ask my great-great-grandfather, "I've heard a story about a ghettoite who received a large inheritance recently from an aunt he hardly even knew. Is this true?"

"Well, yes and no," replied Grandpa, laughing. "You mean Reb Shmolskit. An inheritance he did receive, but a lot of money it was not. In fact, there was no money at all. A few months ago a traveling man came from a distant village—I think it was Divornekov—and told Reb Shmolskit that his aunt had died and left him a handsome brooch, which he had brought. That was it. The man said Shmolskit's aunt had died penniless and had been buried in a pauper's grave. I saw the brooch; it is handsome, perhaps, but isn't silver or gold, just rusty old tin decorated with chunks of colored glass. Shmolskit's 'inheritance' has no value beyond sentiment, I can assure you. In fact, I believe he sold it to one of his neighbors for a few kopeks, and she gave it to her nephew's bride."

The next day it was discovered that the Siberian

stranger had disappeared, vanished—*poof!*—into thin air. Now the ghettoites' suspicion was truly aroused. Who was he really? Where had he come from, and where could he have gone so quickly? It was a field day for Shmulke-Levika and others of her ilk. By the time she'd told the story a few times, the mysterious stranger had become a werewolf, transformed by the magic of Chavisteris, the great Siberian wizard, into an ersatz wandering Jew, doomed to wander with the phases of the moon in endless torment until.... Shmulke-Levika could go on and on like that. And for a long time, that's what most of the ghettoites believed.

Then at last the true story of the Siberian stranger came to light. One day several months later, Rabbi Shmul went to town and happened to meet Captain Magirkik of the regional police, with whom he was on friendly terms. He invited the captain to join him in a glass of schnapps, and as they drank a rare smile slowly drifted across the captain's stern face. "So, I hear you have had a visit from a Jew from Siberia," he said.

"Yes, we have," answered the rabbi, "and a curious thing it was, too. The man showed up one day from out of nowhere. He stayed only two or three days, and then he disappeared. He never even said goodbye."

The captain burst into loud guffaws. "That's rich, that is! That man wasn't Siberian. He's never even seen Siberia. He's not a Jew either. He's a tax inspector from Moscow! His name is Jamikek, he's been a friend of mine for years, and he told me the whole story. Some lady he met on a train told him that one of your men had inherited a fortune, and he went to investigate, disguised as a Jew—he even looks a little like a Jew, don't you think? He wanted to make an example of this tax-evader. But the story turned out to be phony. Jamikek told me he spoke to the rabbi—that must have been you—who told him that all the guy got was a lousy tin brooch. And boy, Jamikek was mad as a wet cat. He'd made his department spend money for train fare and whatnot, all on a bogus case. He was so mad he wanted to arrest that loudmouthed lady who told him the story in the first place. But I talked him out of it, and finally he decided to just let it drop."

Rabbi Shmul was astounded. He'd suspected something was amiss, but he shuddered now to think how close Shmulke-Levika had come to getting Reb Shmolskit, herself, and perhaps even Shmul arrested. But he decided not to tell anyone the true story. After all, it was the czar's tax inspector who had been duped, and he chuckled to himself as he reflected how a ghetto yenta had foiled the government of the czar.

The Running-Jumping Rooster

IT ALL STARTED when Shames Drayzuch agreed to let Froy Chana-Petzik decorate the succah one year. Every fall, during the Succoth harvest festival, the ghettoites always erected a community succah, a small hut, on the grounds of the shul to represent the temporary dwellings used by the Jews during their exile in the wilderness. Unlike some other ghettos, where each family put up its own succah, in Orsha they built just the one, and any family who wished to could use it for a traditional Succoth meal. In all other respects, however, the Orsha succah was the same as any other. It was built of old scraps of wood and partially roofed over with branches, leaving plenty of gaps so those inside could see the stars and the moon in the sky. It was decorated with flowers, fruits of the season, and even small trees, all joyfully celebrating the bounty of the harvest.

Despite all the decoration, and despite all the hammering and nailing of the shames and his helpers, the succah was every bit the ramshackle hut it was supposed to be, a fit representative of the desert hovels of yore. One year, in fact, during the tenure of Rabbi Shlomo, Shmul's father, a huge storm with high winds made its uninvited way into Orsha and blew the succah down, scattering bits of wood and decorations everywhere. The ghettoites were frightened at first, thinking that this calamity represented the wrath of G-d against them for some unknown sin that some one among them had committed. But Rabbi Shlomo explained that it was just G-d's way of reminding the Jews of the frail transience of worldly existence, and emphasizing to them that faith must be built on a firm foundation, not thrown together like a clapboard shack, or it would be blown apart by the first wind of doubt.

Each year, after the succah had been built, the shames appointed one of the ghetto women as the chief decorator, and to her fell the happy task of gathering from the ghetto families the flowers, fruits, and branches that would adorn the succah. Well, one year he made the mistake of appointing Froy Chana-Petzik, and that's when the trouble started.

Chana-Petzik had her own ideas about things. She was a strong-willed woman who would not be denied. She always had her way with her husband, Reb Histek, the nebech who sewed buttons at the clothing factory. And she never did anything by halves. To decorate the succah, fruits and flowers were not enough for her. No, she needed something more extravagant, something that would outdo all the succoth of the past, and so she decided to bring half a dozen of the baby chicks she always raised and let them range about the succah as a kind of living decoration. These chicks were her pride and joy and were the one of the mainstays of her household. When they were grown they would provide eggs, meat, and a few cash sales to supplement Reb Histek's meager wages from button-sewing. And although the family was as poor as anyone in the ghetto, having a few chickens in the yard gave their house a look of prosperity. Now Chana-Petzik stood back proudly as she watched the tiny yellow fluffballs pecking happily about the yard around the succah.

When Shames Drayzuch saw the chicks in the shul yard, he almost laid an egg himself. "What in the world are these chicks doing at our temple?" he demanded. But Froy Chana-Petzik retorted, "They're my chicks, and they're part of the decoration. After all, Shames, baby chicks are part of the harvest, too, aren't they?" There was no denying it, and no gainsaying Chana-Petzik, and so the shames let her have her way; after all, it would only be for a few days.

But he should have known better, and so should she. For the autumn nights were often quite cold, especially during the year Chana-Petzik decorated the succah, and the flimsy roof with its gaping holes provided scant protection from the frost. In her zeal Chana-Petzik had overlooked the temporary nature of the succah. She had forgotten that it represented a time of hardship, and never considered that baby chicks aren't used to much hardship, or that the Jews wandering in the desert might not have kept chickens at all. And so on their very first night of symbolic exile in the succah, Chana-Petzik's prized baby chicks froze to death, and the shames found the poor things there in the morning, their fine yellow down decorated with frost.

Chana-Petzik was distraught over the loss not only of her prized decorations but also of her investment. The one rooster she and her husband owned had grown old and derelict in his duties, and those six chicks were a blessing that would not likely come again. As soon as she had disposed of their tiny corpses, she began nagging Reb Histek about buying a new rooster.

"That old rooster's no good anymore," she complained. "He isn't doing his job, and our chickens are unhappy. They lay fewer eggs, and go around all day scratching the ground looking for tomorrow. I can hear them crying because that old rooster pays them no attention. And where will we get fresh eggs and meat next year? You must go buy us a new rooster."

"Yes, dear," said Reb Histek, anxious as ever to appease his wife before her temper rose. He did all he could to please her, working late every Thursday to have enough money to give her for shabbes dinner every week, and doing chores around the house before she had a chance to yell at him for neglecting them. But it was she who handled the family's money, and she who made decisions about how to spend it. In a way, Histek felt like that old wornout, hen-pecked rooster himself.

"B-but if we have a good rooster," he asked timorously, "won't all our eggs become fertile? And then they won't be kosher anymore, so how can we eat them?"

"Gay klop kop in vant! (Go bang your head against the wall!)" she said, using her favorite expression. "Don't worry me with your mishegoss! I wouldn't feed you trayf, you poor ninny. But we must have new baby chicks, and there's only one place they come from."

"B-but where will we get the money to pay for a new rooster?"

"Here," Chana-Petzik said, handing him a coin. "I've saved a whole ruble from my household money—don't ask where it came from, because it sure didn't come from button-sewing!"

"B-but where do I find such a rooster?"

"I've heard of a goy, a Russian named Ivan Something-or-other, who lives in Grendlik and who sells roosters and chickens. You go to him and see if he won't sell you one."

"But that's ten kilometers away," Reb Histek

complained. "It's a long walk. And how will I find this Ivan if I don't know his last name? There must be a million goyim named Ivan."

"Gay klop kop in vant!" she said again. "Just go to Grendlik like I tell you, and ask around. The walk will do you good. Don't lose that ruble, and don't let him cheat you! And don't come back without a rooster. Now go, already!"

So Histek, holding the ruble firmly in his hand, set out on the road that ran west from Orsha to Grendlik. It was a rare adventure for him, for he had only been outside Orsha two or three times before. Forgetting his errand, he stopped to sniff the flowers and admire the scenery along the way. It was a beautiful day, one of those crisp autumn mornings that make the blood race in one's veins. By and by he came to a brook, and he lay on his stomach and drank some of its cool, delicious water, a treat he would long remember, and as he left he looked forward to drinking there again on his way home.

After a few hours Histek reached Grendlik, which turned out to be a very small village with no Jews and no ghetto. This worried him. Perhaps the Russian people here weren't friendly to Jews; perhaps they'd set their dogs on him. Cautiously, he approached a passer-by and asked in his very best Russian where he might find someone by the name of Ivan.

"Ivan who?" said the man. "If you're not particular, you can pretty much take your choice of any house in the village."

"Ivan who sells chickens," explained Histek, hoping the description would suffice.

"Oh, him!" said the man. "You'll find his farm at the western edge of the village. But if you're going to do business with him, be careful, because he loves to cheat his customers."

This was not encouraging. The passerby seemed friendly enough, but this guy Ivan sounded like trouble. Maybe he was a hater of Jews. Oh well, Histek thought, Ivan couldn't really cheat him too badly if he only had a single ruble, and so he continued on.

At the edge of town he came to a farm where a tall, husky man was shoveling manure into piles. "Are you Ivan?" he asked.

The man looked up and carefully scrutinized Histek. "Who wants to know?" he said.

"M-my name is Histek," said Histek, "and I've come from Orsha to buy a rooster."

The man stared at him for a minute, then said "Ivan's inside," and returned to his work.

This Ivan must really be something, thought Histek. Maybe he was the Ivan the Terrible he'd heard so much about. But then he thought of Chana-Petzik at home and heard her shouting "Gay klop kop in vant"; maybe this time she really would make him bang his head against the wall. He walked to the house and knocked timidly on the door.

"Come in, dammit, whoever you are!" called a gruff voice, and Histek tentatively pushed the door open and entered. Inside was a huge man, almost two meters tall, corpulent but muscular, with a bald head and burly, brawny arms. His pale blue eyes stared out of deep sockets like mad hornets as he sized up Histek. "Who the hell are you?" he demanded.

"I-I'm Histek, from Orsha, and my wife has sent me to buy a rooster. See, she gave me the money." He held out his hand with the ruble in it for Ivan to see.

Ivan's manner changed immediately when he saw the coin. "Ah, come in, friend. Yes, I'll sell you a rooster. How much do you have to spend?"

A question like that would have put any experienced bargain hunter on his toes, but Histek had no experience whatever at bargaining, and he was merely relieved to hear that the man would sell him a rooster and not kill him on the spot. "One ruble," he answered honestly.

"Ah, one ruble," repeated Ivan. "Well, you've come to the right place, friend. I just happen to have a genuine running-jumping rooster that I'm sure you'll like. I suppose you know all about running-jumping roosters. They're the best kind, you know."

Histek didn't know anything about any kind of rooster, but he knew enough not to give himself away. "Oh, yes, of course," he blathered. "A running-jumping rooster is just what I hoped to find."

"Well, you're a man who knows his roosters. I'm sure your wife will be overjoyed when you come home with a runner-jumper," said Ivan slyly. "But I'm afraid the price is one ruble, three kopeks. Are you sure you don't have a little more money to spend?"

Histek was terrified. He saw the running-jumping rooster vanish before his eyes, taking his domestic tranquility with it; but just then he remembered the two kopeks he had sewn into the cuff of his trousers to hide them from his wife. "Oh, yes!" he said, "I do have another two kopeks, but I'm afraid that's really all I have."

"Well, you're a hard bargainer," said Ivan. "I'll sell you the running-jumping rooster for one ruble, two kopeks, but only if you promise not to mention the price to anyone."

Histek agreed immediately. He was flattered, and he was proud that he had saved a whole kopek through his bargaining skill. He held out his money for Ivan to take. Certainly, he would never tell anyone—least of all would he tell Chana-Petzik about the extra two kopeks.

Ivan took the money and led Histek out to a small pen behind the barn, where he snatched up a handsome rooster with brightly colored tail feathers. "Yes, sir," he said, "this here is a genuine running-jumping rooster. He's good and lively, so feed him well and he'll stay that way. But be careful not to let him loose, or you'll have the devil's own time catching him." He handed the rooster to Histek, who tried to take it in his arms like a baby. "No, not like that," said Ivan. "That might do for a regular rooster, but not for a running-jumping rooster. You gotta hold him like this," he said, passing the bird's upturned legs to Histek. "Hold his legs tight, and keep his head pointed down so he don't flap. There you go."

Histek took the rooster by the legs and thanked Ivan, then set off back down the road to Orsha, proud of his purchase. It was a fine-looking running-jumping rooster, indeed, he thought. And it was a feisty one, too; every once in a while it would lift its head and start squawking and flapping its wings like the Cossacks were after it. But Histek just held on tighter, and pretty soon he got the hang of pushing its head down until the bird went limp like rag.

By the time they reached the brook, Histek was very thirsty and his hand was starting to cramp up. The rooster had been so quiet Histek thought it must be asleep, and he thought he would take a chance and lay the bird down while he rested and took a drink.

It was a bad mistake. As soon as the rooster touched the ground it jumped up with a shriek and a flurry of wings that knocked Histek on his kiester, and took off as though it had been shot from a cannon. Thoughts of that cool drink vanished from Histek's mind; he ran after the crazed running-jumping rooster as it proved its name up and down the creek, darting from one bush to another, first on one bank, then on the other. Histek stayed close on its tail, but he couldn't seem to get close enough to nab it. Finally the rooster made a false lunge, and Histek made a daring leap and landed right on top of the bird, pinning it under his chest.

Fortunately, neither man nor fowl was hurt, but now Histek knew what a running-jumping rooster was. He forgot all about his drink of water and didn't let go of the bird again until he reached his home and handed it to his wife.

Chana-Petzik held up the bird and examined it skeptically. "Is this the best rooster that cheater would give you? What kind of rooster is this, anyway?"

"It's a genuine running-jumping rooster," said Histek enthusiastically, kvelling with new ornithological knowledge, "and you ought to see him go."

"A running-jumping rooster, huh?" said his wife, "Gay klop kop in vant! I just hope he runs after my hens and jumps on them. Did you get any change?"

Histek didn't dare tell his wife he had spent an extra two kopeks when she already seemed satisfied—as satisfied as she ever got, anyway, so why spoil it? They carried the rooster to the hen house and locked it in for the night, Chana-Petzik explaining that it had to learn where it lived. They went indoors and had a small supper, then retired for the evening.

But the next morning when they let the rooster out into the yard with the chickens, Chana-Petzik immediately learned what a running-jumping rooster could do. The bird bolted from the hen house and made straight for the low fence separating their yard from that of their neighbors, Reb Shistokov and his wife, Becka. In one graceful leap it cleared the fence like it wasn't even there. It alighted on the other side, looked around pompously, and gave a brazen "cock-a-doodle-doo," then began scratching the ground for crumbs alongside the neighbor's chickens.

Shistokov and Becka heard the rooster's crow and came out to see what was going on, and when they saw the strange rooster in their yard they immediately tried to shoo it back over the fence.

"Get that damned rooster back in your own yard!" Reb Shistokov shouted at Histek.

"We don't need any trayf eggs!" added Becka as she fetched the running-jumping intruder a good kick that put him back on his own turf.

Chana-Petzik ran after the rooster until she was breathless, but she couldn't catch him. Finally she and Histek together cornered it by the outhouse, and Histek threw his jacket over it. They locked it up in the hen house and didn't let it out again for two days. "That'll teach him where he belongs— and what will happen if he runs away again!" declared Chana-Petzik.

But when they finally let it out again, the rooster was hell-bent for revenge. In one motion he was up and over the fence, and with a taunting crow he joined Becka's hens in their breakfast.

Again Reb Shistokov and Becka came running, she with a broom and he with an axe. "Keep that no-good rooster out of our yard or we'll kill him!" shouted Becka. "It'll be your fault if our eggs are fertilized, and who's going to replace them? You? Feh! I don't think so." Becka swung the broom hard and sent the running-jumping rooster flying back over the fence, where Reb Histek and Chana-Petzik chased it around until they caught it and returned it again to the hen house.

"Running-jumping rooster!" spat Chana-Petzik. "I'll give you running and jumping!" and she took after Reb Histek and chased *him* around the yard for a while.

This time they left the rooster cooped up for a week. But as soon as they released it, it was back over the fence, and Becka was again threatening to kill it. "It obviously prefers our yard to yours, and frankly it's not hard to see why. If it wants to belong to us, why that's fine. I'll call the shochet in the morning!"

"Gay klop kop in vant!" countered Chana-Petzik. "You touch one feather on that bird and I'll call for the police!"

They caught the rooster again and locked it up, but that didn't stop the yelling back and forth across the fence. The neighbors, who had once been friends, were now sworn enemies, and all because of a meshugge rooster. Histek didn't dare let it out again; there would be blood shed, for sure—maybe even his own. But they couldn't just keep it locked up all the time; it would pine away and die. There seemed to be no solution to the dilemma of the running-jumping rooster, and the neighbors finally agreed to take the matter to Rabbi Shmul, the one person whose advice both parties would accept.

The very next day the two couples went to my great-great-grandfather's house, and after Helga had laid out the tea and mandelbrot they began to recount the tale—Becka complaining that the rooster would make their eggs inedible, Reb Shistokov threatening to kill it, Chana-Petzik protesting the abuse her neighbors had heaped on her just because of a stupid rooster, and Reb Histek explaining that this was no ordinary barnyard fowl but a genuine running-jumping rooster, that it was very valuable, and that it would eventually learn where it belonged.

Rabbi Shmul listened carefully and tried not to laugh, lifting his teacup to his lips to hide his smile. When each of the parties had vented their steam, he laid his cup aside and thoughtfully clasped his hands under his chin.

"Froy Chana-Petzik," he began, "how high is the fence between the two yards?"

"Maybe a meter," she guessed.

But Becka jumped in to have her say. "A meter? Feh! Maybe half a meter, no more."

Rabbi Shmul considered this. "And, Reb Histek, how high can this running-jumping rooster jump?"

"Oh, very high, Rabbi," said Histek proudly. "At least a meter and a half."

"Then I have the solution to your problem," my great-great-grandfather announced. "The fence must be raised to two whole meters. And to make sure everyone is satisfied, I suggest that both husbands work together to assure themselves that the fence will be high enough that the rooster will not be able to jump over it. This is the only way that Chana-Petzik can raise her chicks and Becka can eat her infertile eggs in peace."

Everyone agreed to the plan, although neither of the women seemed wholly confident of it. After the holiday the men took down the dilapidated succah—the same one that had been the final home of Chana-Petzik's chicks—and with the old boards they began to build up the fence. They built it two and a half meters high, just to be sure, while their wives stood by and kibitzed.

"This better work," said Becka, "or we'll be having chicken Kiev for dinner tonight!"

"Gay klop kop in vant!" retorted Chana-Petzik. "Just make sure the fence is high enough and it will work, all right."

In fact, the new fence seemed to work well. Every morning and twice every afternoon, the running-jumping rooster would take a flying leap at the fence, dashing himself at it again and again until he was exhausted. But he never was able to jump over it. Even several months later he was still at it, but he remained in Chana-Petzik's yard where he belonged.

Eventually fragile peace settled over the neighborhood. At Chanukah Chana-Petzik candled eight eggs to make sure they weren't fertile, and brought them to Becka and Shistokov as a gift, and on the new year Becka reciprocated with a delicious chicken stew. They were friends once again, and in the end it was only the running-jumping rooster who klopped his head against the wall that separated the two yards.

The Unhappy Chanukah

BECAUSE THE CELEBRATION of Chanukah occurs during the Jewish month of Kislev, usually the Gregorian month of December, unlearned Russians sometimes referred to it as the "Jewish Christmas." Nothing could be further from the truth. Christmas, as everyone knows, is a religious holiday commemorating the birth of Jesus; Chanukah, on the other hand, is a secular holiday marking the victory of the Jews and the Maccabees over the Syrians, who had attempted to convert them forcibly to Greek polytheism. When the Jews had retaken their temple from the Syrians, they relit the eternal flame that burned before the holy Ark of the Covenant; they had only one day's supply of oil for the lamp, and dispatched runners to bring more as quickly as possible. But by a miracle, when the runners returned eight days later the eternal flame was still burning. And that is why the celebration of Chanukah lasts eight days.

An eight-day holiday is a wonderful time for visiting with friends and family, rejoicing, giving, and sharing. Unfortunately, eight days also allow plenty of time for trouble to arise, as it did one particular year in the ghetto of Orsha.

The first night of the holiday was bitterly cold. The wind was blowing a gale, and a light rain had started to fall. The shames, Reb Drayzuch, had gone early to the shul to light the stoves, so that when the congregants arrived it would be warm and comfortable. Everything was ready, and he checked again to make sure that all would be perfect at the service. The beautiful shiny brass menorah, which had been made the previous year by a somewhat inebriated metalsmith in Smolensk after the shames accidentally broke the old pewter one, stood proudly upon the lectern. Its first candle was in place, ready to be lit, and the shames candle was standing ready to light it. The shames was pleased. Everything would go smooth as silk tonight.

Family by family, the ghettoites came in out of the blustery night. They shrugged off their heavy fur coats, unwrapped their thick mufflers, and took their seats in the neat rows of benches and extra chairs the shames had put out that morning. When everyone was settled Rabbi Shmul went to the lectern and started the service with prayers for the lighting of the menorah, and Shames Drayzuch carefully lit the shames candle. Slowly and ceremoniously, he brought its flame to the candle that represented the first night of the holiday and touched the flame to the wick. The fire passed from candle to candle, and the shames felt a warm glow spread inside himself and throughout the congregation as the tiny light began to burn. But then all of a sudden the flame sputtered, and with an audible sizzle it winked out.

Unperturbed, or at least acting unperturbed, Reb Drayzuch picked up the shames candle again. It would take more than a recalcitrant taper to spoil his meticulous Chanukah plans. Very carefully he relit the first-night candle, but no sooner was it lit than it again went *pzzzilt!* and died.

The shames scratched his beard and wrinkled his brow as he relit the candle a third time. Maybe he shouldn't have bought the cheap candles, he thought; maybe he should replace it. But just as the candle sputtered to life, the flame went *fzzthp!* and went out again.

Now the shames was concerned, and a low murmur spread through the congregation. Was this an omen? What dire event could such a mysterious sign portend? Had someone in the congregation sinned so awfully that G-d—blessed be his holy name!—would not allow the ghettoites to celebrate Chanukah? The congregants began to feel suspicious, and they all sat up straight and tried to look innocent.

The shames' hand shook as he brought the shames candle to the wick again. But then he noticed a wetness at the base of the menorah, and just then a drop of water fell on the back of his hand. He looked up at the rafters as another drop fell and landed smack on his nose. There between the boards was a dark water stain, at the center of which a big drop of rainwater hung precariously for a moment before it let go and fell *plop* into the shames's eye. It was no omen; the roof was leaking!

The shames closed his eyes and made a little prayer of thanks, then moved the menorah a few inches to the left—to the south, an inch or two closer to Jerusalem—and the service continued uninterrupted by further ill portents.

Two days later another small problem arose—not a problem, really, but a moral dilemma. Rabbi Shmul was eating his simple breakfast of salt fish with bread and tea when there was a knock on the door. He went to open it himself, and found Reb Yiskilik, a local farmer, standing nervously in the doorway.

"Happy Chanukah," the rabbi greeted him. But Yiskilik didn't look very happy.

"Rabbi," he asked shyly, "may I speak with you a moment?"

"Of course," said Shmul. "Come in, come in." He led Yiskilik to the table and brought out another glass. "What's on your mind, my friend?" he asked.

"Well, you see, Rabbi," Yiskilik stammered, "it's about the holiday. My wife and I, we want to observe Chanukah properly, and we want to make sure our children learn correctly what the holiday is about. So we have our menorah at home, and every night we gather around to light the next candle, just like our parents taught us to do.

"But…but what about this Chanukah gelt?"

Even back then, despite the poverty of the ghetto, it was traditional for parents to give their children small coins in honor of the holiday. But Reb Yiskilik seemed troubled by this custom.

"Chanukah is supposed to be a holy occasion, isn't it?" he asked. "And is it not true that on holy days we may not handle money? So how is it that we may give Chanukah gelt to our children? Isn't this practice irreligious?"

Rabbi Shmul smiled under his beard. Reb Yiskilik was a devout man, to be sure; but the rabbi had also heard that last winter he had lost much of his crop of rye to weevils, and he wondered if that might be behind his question.

"No, my friend," my great-great-grandfather gently replied, "there is nothing improper about giving Chanukah gelt. Chanukah is not really a religious holiday at all. True, it celebrates the winning of our religious freedom; but it is not listed in our Torah or described in our Bible. Therefore there is no problem in handling money during Chanukah.

"But," he added, hoping it might help, "it should be only very small amounts of money. We wouldn't want to encourage our children to become avaricious. Chanukah should be a time of sharing what we have, even if it isn't much; it is not just an opportunity to get all the gifts you can. So really a few kopeks are actually a better gift than many rubles."

Reb Yiskilik smiled and rose from the table. "Thank you, Rabbi," he said. "You've certainly helped our family quite a bit." As Yiskilik left, Shmul was glad to see that he seemed relieved—although, the rabbi thought to himself, perhaps not so relieved as he had hoped to be.

🙦

Serious trouble did not rear its head until the fifth day of the holiday. Rabbi Shmul and my great-great-grandmother Helga had just lit the fifth candle in their menorah at home when there was a knock on the door. Expecting holiday visitors, Helga ran to answer, and she was surprised to find Captain Magirkik of the police with his hat in his hand.

The captain was an old friend of the rabbi and his wife. Like many Russian civil servants and bureaucrats, he was really just a mild-mannered man who wanted no trouble, and Shmul and Helga had always been very helpful in keeping the ghettoites out of trouble in the first place. Now, however, the dark look on his face told them that this was not just a friendly holiday visit.

"I'm sorry to bother you on the holiday, but I've come on a small matter of business," the captain said as he stamped the snow from his boots and came in. "A messenger has just arrived from Moscow with bad news. I don't know how to tell you this, but I'm afraid I am here to arrest you." There was a very awkward silence, and the captain was obviously embarrassed. "Believe me, Rabbi, I have no idea what this is all about, but I'm afraid I have to do my duty and place you under house arrest."

Shmul and Helga were dumbfounded. "But why, for heaven's sake?" asked Grandpa. "I haven't done anything at all. In fact, we've been celebrating Chanukah for the last four days, and I haven't even left the ghetto!"

The captain heaved a deep sigh. "I'm so sorry, Rabbi," he said, "but I really haven't a clue. I asked the messenger, but he didn't know either. His only message to me was 'arrest the rabbi.' He said he thought he would be back in a few days with more information, but in the meantime I must command you not to leave this house."

"Why, this must be some mistake," protested Helga.

"I'm sure it must be," apologized Captain Magirkik, "and I know everything will be all right as soon as we can get this straightened out. But for now I really have no choice."

"But Captain," pleaded Rabbi Shmul, "I'm supposed to lead the Chanukah services at the shul tomorrow. May I at least do that?"

"Well, okay," agreed Magirkik. "I know I can trust you. But come home immediately after the service is over, and try not to let anybody see you come and go." With that the captain sighed again and took his leave, promising to return as soon as there was news.

Two days later the captain returned to Rabbi Shmul's house as promised. When Helga let him in she and Grandpa could see that although he was blushing deeply he was visibly relieved, and he stuttered as he began his explanation.

"Rabbi, Rebbitsin, I'm truly sorry," he began. "Just as we all suspected, there has been a dreadful mistake. The messenger, it seems, got his instructions wrong. You see, in the village of Bialikik, about twenty kilometers north of here, there is an Arab man who has been trying to stir up dissent among the Moslems and trying to get them to rebel against the czar and to set up a Moslem state. This, of course, the czar cannot allow, and so the messenger was sent to order the arrest of the *Arab,* not the *rabbi.* Since he was just a messenger they didn't bother to tell him why the arrest was being made; in fact, they didn't give him any information at all, so he had no way of figuring out that he'd misunderstood *rabbi* for *Arab.* He passed on the same order to me, and I had no choice but to do my duty. I hope you understand, Rabbi, Rebbitsin, and I hope you'll accept my apology, for I have nothing else to offer you; and I hope this won't affect our friendship."

Of course they understood. Minor officials of the czar's government had little more say over their lives than did the Jews in the ghetto—probably less—and Shmul and Helga were sympathetic to their friend the captain. He was, after all, only a pawn in the czar's cruel games, just as they were themselves. Helga put on water for tea and brought out a fresh loaf of mandelbrot, and by the time the captain left they were all laughing together over the incident. Rabbi Shmul went to the service at the shul that evening as planned, and he lingered for a while afterward to talk to the people, grateful for the little freedom he enjoyed. But in the back of his mind as he surveyed all the problems this Chanukah season had brought, he thought, What next?

What next, indeed? The very next night, at two o'clock in the morning of the last night of Chanukah, Rabbi Shmul was awakened by someone hammering loudly at the front door and shouting "Rabbi! Rabbi Shmul!"

Hoping the noise would not awaken his wife, Shmul quickly threw on his dressing gown, descended the steps from the sleeping loft, and opened the door to admit Pikilek ben Halavek, who was as wide-eyed as Shmul was groggy.

"Rabbi, please come quickly," he panted. "It's the baby!"

G-d help us, thought Shmul. Just a few years earlier he had married Reb Pikilek and Gitella-Luva, and everyone in the ghetto knew she was now pregnant and due any time. Gitella was a tiny woman, and she had grown so huge it seemed she would burst. Rabbi Shmul wasn't the only ghettoite who feared for her and for her baby, and now with Pikilek standing breathlessly on his doorstep, the rabbi feared the worst.

He followed the agitated husband out into the night, and they began trudging as fast as they could through the snow toward Pikilek's house. The sky was clear and black, the moon cast an enchanting glow on the deep snow, and the air was bitterly cold. Shmul clutched his dressing gown about him and huffed and puffed as he struggled to keep up with the frantic Pikilek. The worst scenarios played out in his mind. It must be serious; otherwise they would have called the midwife, not the rabbi. What if Gitella could not deliver? What if the birth were breech? What if—but no, better not even think of that!

At last they reached Pikilek's house, a small shack almost buried in a deep blue-white snow drift. "This way, Rabbi, this way," urged Pikilek as he showed him directly into the bedroom. There, sitting up in bed smiling, was Gitella holding a newborn baby gently in her arms. The baby's blanket was pulled back from its face, and the rabbi saw that it was sleeping as blissfully as any child might sleep on the last night of Chanukah.

"Rabbi," said Pikilek proudly, "this is our little Shimmela. He was born just an hour ago. Isn't he beautiful?"

Shmul was relieved, but slowly his perplexity resurfaced. "But why on earth did you pull me out of my bed in the middle of night? Is the baby ill?"

"Oh, heavens no!" said Gitella, the happy mother. "He's fine—in fact, he's wonderful. But Froy Mikeles, the midwife, said you would bless him for us, and so I sent my husband to fetch you. Will you, Rabbi? Will you bless our little boy?"

Oy, vey! thought Grandpa. So that's all it is!

"Of course I'll bless your baby," he sighed, trying not to let his voice betray his irritation. Even a rabbi in a ghetto of Russia in the time of the czars has limits to his patience when he is dragged out of bed in the middle of a cold winter's night. "But at his brith next week, when he is named—not now!"

"Oh," said Gitella.

"Oh," said Pikilek, his face turning red during the awkward pause that followed.

"Forgive me, Rabbi," said the embarrassed mother, "I didn't know. Shimmela is our very first baby, so when Froy Mikeles said you'd bless him, I thought she meant right away. I'm sorry we brought you out for nothing."

"Well, maybe not for nothing," said Grandpa with a smile as he moved closer to get a better look at the child. He was indeed beautiful, plump and pink and sleeping the sleep of the innocent in his mother's arms.

Well, after all, it is Chanukah, Grandpa thought; and perhaps now some good had finally come to this unlucky holiday. And as he slowly trudged home in the snowy cold, his heart at least was warmed.

Now if he could just live through the next day without any more tsouris!

Haman Lives!

As SPRINGTIME BEGAN to warm the frozen fields around the ghetto of Orsha, ghettoites young and old began preparing for Purim, also called the Feast of Lots, one of the favorite and most joyful celebrations of the Jewish calendar. Despite the harsh poverty of most ghetto families, neighbors exchanged whatever gifts they could afford or obtain—flasks of wine, bottles of schnapps, delicious baked goods, and savory smoked meats and fish. Even the merchants of the ghetto pitched in to help the needy; during the rest of the year they counted every ruble and kopek and just barely got by, but as Purim approached they began clearing their shelves of items that hadn't sold well, and although they griped and grumbled as they did so, it was with smiling faces and light hearts that they made generous gifts of food to the many ghettoites whose cupboards were bare after the long Russian winter.

On the eve of the holiday, Rabbi Shmul went to the shul for the reading of the Book of Esther, or the Megillah as it is known to Jews, which recounts the story of a plot to exterminate all the Jews in ancient Persia, a plot hatched by the tyrannical King Ahasuerus' evil prime minister, Haman. This was perhaps Shmul's very favorite among his many rabbinical duties, and was surely a favorite of the rest of the ghettoites as well—especially the children. For as the congregants filed in to the shul, Shames Drayzuch and his wife were ready at the door to hand out noisemakers to all the children, so that as Rabbi Shmul read the awful story of the prime minister's dastardly plot, every time the accursed name Haman was read, the entire room would burst into a cacophony of noise—clacking sticks and shaking rattles, accompanied by hoots, hollers, hisses, and some of the most robust raspberries ever heard on earth—to drive away the very name of the hated schemer.

Fortunately, however, the Jews of Persia were saved by the heroism of the king's wife, Esther, a Jewess, who convinced her husband that Haman's true purpose was to usurp the throne and make himself the ruler of all Persia. In the end it was the evil minister himself who hung from the gibbet he had built with his own hands.

Thus tyranny was defeated by the wisdom of a Jewess, and therein lies the true joy of Purim: for each time the tale is recounted, it is a confirmation that tyrants and fanatics are not omnipotent, but can and will be defeated through patience, reason, love, and faith—and plenty of noise-making! And each time the story is read, tyranny is symbolically booed, hissed, noise-makered, and raspberried right out of existence.

This particular Purim was one of the best anyone could remember. The congregants listened in silent, rapt attention to the rabbi's reading. But when the name of Haman was read, all Gehenna broke loose, and this happened again and again until, by the time the reading was finished, everyone's voice was quite hoarse. But they weren't through with Haman yet! After the service was over, the women served hamantashen, triangular pastries filled with honeyed poppy seeds or mashed prunes, and as the people chewed these delicious morsels they imagined they were masticating the evil prime minister himself. Nor was that all. Some of the ghettoites even wrote the name of the usurper on the soles of their shoes with coal, so that with each step they ground his memory into the dirt.

After the service Rabbi Shmul and Shames Drayzuch stood together in a corner of the shul munching their hamantashen and trying to stay out of the way while the children ran about making as much noise as they could and grinding Haman under their feet. Between bites, the shames said to the rabbi with an ironic smile, "You know, Rabbi, I often wonder how it is that every year, year after year, this Haman is reviled, hanged, and ground underfoot, and yet each year he manages to reappear during Purim to be hanged again."

"Yes, it's true," replied the rabbi, smacking his lips as a wistful smile spread across his face. "But you must remember, Shames, there are many, many Hamans—but only one Purim."

Indeed, there are Hamans everywhere, and it was the very next day that the rabbi heard of another one, for Reb Pripichek appeared at his door with a mournful expression on his face and a doleful tale on his lips.

"Rabbi, I need your advice," he began as they sat down across from each other at the rabbi's table and Helga served them tea and mandelbrot. "You know that my mother-in-law has been living with my wife and me since her husband passed away last year. And, Rabbi, I hate to speak ill of her, but she has given me no peace whatsoever since the day she moved in—in fact, she seems to make it her primary business in life to find fault with whatever I do. For example, sometimes I stop on my way home from work to have a glass of schnapps and some conversation with my friends, just like everyone does. I never drink much, and I never come home drunk, but if my mother-in-law catches even the faintest whiff of schnapps on my breath, she starts in on me like I was the biggest shikker in all of Russia."

"I see," said Rabbi Shmul sympathetically. "Everyone needs the company of his friends; maybe you just need to find a different time or place for it."

"No, Rabbi," protested Pripichek, "it's not just that. If it were, I could live with it. I'm a patient man, you know that. But the torment doesn't stop there. Every night after we eat our little supper, I like to sit down with my children and listen to their lessons. I ask the boys what you've taught them that day, and I ask my daughter what she learned from the rebbitsin. That's my duty as a father, isn't it? And it's about the only time I get to spend with the children at all. But it's not good enough for my mother-in-law. She starts in on me right in front of the children: Why do I sit around doing nothing? Why can't I help my wife instead of making her wash all the dishes and do all the work? I'm good for nothing, she says, a lazy, wasteful shlemiel.

"But that's still not all. If she can find no other cause for criticism, she complains about how little money I make. I'm the laziest shnorrer in the ghetto, in all Russia—in all creation, if you listen to her.

"And as if all that weren't enough, now she's turned my wife, Puppa, against me. Puppa never complained before if I stopped on my way home; but now that her mother's come to live with us, every time I am a little bit late Puppa screams at me as though I'd been out painting the ghetto red. Well, it could use a coat of paint, let's face it, but I'm hardly a carouser, Rabbi. She used to love to hear me going over lessons with our little ones; but now she waves her dishpan hands in my face and complains. And at the end of the week when I bring home my pay, it's never enough. How can she feed the family on what's left after I've drunk half of it on my way home, she says?

"Rabbi, I'm at my wit's end. Yes, I'm patient; but Job I am not. I'm about to call the shochet to take care of that woman, Rabbi. Please tell me, what can I do?"

What indeed, thought the Rabbi. Pripichek wasn't the first man to have a nagging, domineering mother-in-law, and G-d knows he won't be the last. But what advice could he offer this poor tormented man? He couldn't tell Pripichek to turn his mother-in-law out of the house—where would the poor old woman go? And it was probably too late for Pripichek to resolve the matter with his wife; apparently she had begun to side with her mother, and there was too much emotion involved now for an honest discussion, anyway.

"My friend," Shmul said after much though, "I don't think there is anything at all you can do—at least not by yourself. But maybe I can still help. Ask your wife to come see me tomorrow; maybe I can intervene. But please, don't tell her you've been to see me; and above all, if she and her mother start in again tonight, do your best to hold your tongue."

Pripichek promised to do as the rabbi instructed, and he left with a vague feeling of hopefulness. When he had gone Rabbi Shmul turned to his dear wife, Helga, his hands spread wide and a helpless look in his eyes as if to ask "what can I do?" and she gave him an understanding smile.

The next morning Puppa arrived at Smul's house. "You wanted to see me, Rabbi?" she asked.

"Yes, please come in," he said, ushering her to the same chair in which Pripichek had sat the night before.

"Froy Puppa," he began, "I have a problem to discuss with you that is not an easy one to talk about, much less to solve, so please bear with me and try to understand.

"It is good to have a big family and for all of the members of the family to be close to one another. We just celebrated Purim, a time for the whole family to enjoy, and it was wonderful, wasn't it, to have children, parents and grandparents, sisters and brothers, uncles and aunts, all together for the celebration. What could be happier?

"But there comes a time when children grow up and have to leave their parents' homes and begin families of their own. Why? Because they have become adults: they have their own ways of doing things, their own ways of thinking, their own likes and dislikes. When we are children we owe everything to our parents, and our allegiance to them is very clear; but sooner or later every child goes his or her own way.

"Think how it would be if we lived in our parents' houses all our lives. We wouldn't be able to set up our own households or manage our own time or priorities. We couldn't say what we really thought, couldn't express all we really felt, because with all those people around someone would surely take offense at something. We wouldn't be able to devote ourselves to our children and spouses, as it is our duty to do. There would be so many relatives around we'd hardly have a moment to ourselves, and we'd always have to bow to someone else's wishes.

"Now, Froy Puppa, you are married, and you and your husband are as one person in your wedlock. You and he are dependent on each other, and your children, in turn, are dependent on you. And that is as it should be—as it must be, in fact, for your first duty is to your husband and children.

"For the last year your mother has been living with you. And I must say it is a very generous thing you and your husband do in allowing her to take shelter under your roof so that she will not be alone in her widowhood. You must make many sacrifices for her; for example, you must set another place at the table, and fill her plate with food even if it means your own plate is less full than before.

"But the one thing you must never sacrifice for her—nor for anyone—is your duty to your own family and the happiness of your husband and your children. G-d wills it to be so when you take the marriage vows.

"Froy Puppa, I'm afraid it has come to that. Your husband is a patient man, but you mustn't let your mother take advantage of that special quality of his. You mustn't let her criticize him; he is a hardworking and honest man, and he does what he can to make your life and the lives of your children as comfortable as possible. You mustn't let her speak ill of him in front of the children, for they are very impressionable and don't know when to believe what they hear and when not to believe. And when you and your husband decide what you feel is best for your children, your mustn't let her interfere. It is *your* family, after all, and if you and Reb Pripichek are not the heads of your own household, chaos will surely follow.

"But above all, you mustn't allow yourself to be caught in the middle of strife between your husband and your mother. If you treat him harshly, your entire family will suffer. If you allow your mother's criticism to sway you, you will have defaulted on your duty as a wife and a mother. If there is doubt or an argument, it is your duty to take his side, just as it is always his duty to side with you. As I said before, you and your husband are as one person—and how can a person be happy if he is divided against himself?

"Froy Puppa, this problem is not a new one, nor is it peculiar to your family. It has been with us for many, many generations, and it will continue to plague us as long as human beings grow up, leave the home, and begin families of their own. But with patience and understanding—and most of all, with love—you can solve this problem. Please try to understand. You are a brilliant woman, Froy Puppa; please try."

It was a long and delicate speech, and when it

was over Rabbi Shmul's throat felt dry. Puppa
hadn't said a word, but when the rabbi had finished
she nodded her head slowly in what seemed to be
understanding and agreement. She arose and
thanked the rabbi and took her leave. Maybe it will
help, the rabbi thought; but deep inside he had his
doubts. Could Puppa stand up to her mother?
Could her mother change her ways now that she
was living under her daughter's roof?

The answer came only seconds later; in fact, the
knock on the door came so quickly after Puppa had
left that Rabbi Shmul almost thought time was
running backwards, and before he knew what was
happening, Puppa's mother, all one hundred kilos
of her, burst into the room like a tornado in a
house-dress. Without even pausing to say shalom,
she launched into a tirade of accusations and choice
Yiddish epithets that would have scorched the fur
off a wild bear, shouting as though to deafen everyone in the house who might not be deaf already.

"What have you been telling my daughter?" she
demanded. "You've turned her against me with
your vicious lies! You should grow like an onion,
with your head in the ground—that's about the
level of your intelligence—and beets should grow in
your belly! Who do you think you are, Rabbi
Shmabbi, interfering in our lives? Who asked you
to be the ghetto buttinski? Leave that business to
Shmulke the yenta, and go mind your own! You
and your Rebbitsin Schmebbitsin can take a nice
long trip to hell—and on a slow boat, and suffer the
entire trip!"

And with that the rampaging mother-in-law stormed back out again, the door slamming shut in her wake so hard it almost broke the windows.

When she was gone the silence was so loud it made Rabbi Shmul's hair stand on end, and his eyes were as big as saucers. Slowly he turned to Helga and, with a weak smile, spread his hands. "I tried," he said. "That's all I can do, try."

"Nu," said Helga with a consoling smile, "you know as well as I do, my love: there are many, many Hamans—but only one Purim!"

Days of Awe

IT WAS DURING the so-called Days of Awe, the ten days between Rosh Hashanah and Yom Kippur, that diphtheria raged through the ghetto of Orsha. Uninvited, unannounced, and most unwelcome, it burst into the ghetto like a long-lost relative, inflicting itself on nearly half the families, giving the ghettoites a lesson in the frailty of human life that was, in the most literal sense, awful.

The first snows of late autumn had just fallen on the plains of Russia as the people prepared for Rosh Hashanah, the new year celebration. As this happy holiday grew near, the ghettoites greeted each other in the streets with "Leshana tova tikosevu," Hebrew for "May you have a very good year." The Russians of Orsha town thought the Jews must be crazy, celebrating the new year when, according to the Gregorian calendar the Russians used, the old year was only three-quarters done. But the Jews, who used the Hebrew calendar, had their own reasons for celebrating when and as they did.

Rosh Hashanah is not just any new year celebration; it has a lot more meaning than throwing out the old calendar and hanging up a new one. In the Talmud it is written that Rosh Hashanah celebrates not just the birth of a new year, but the birth of the entire world. There are many who believe that the holiday comes during the autumnal month of Tishri because it is a descendant of the ancient Babylonian Day of Judgment—also in the fall—when, the Babylonians believed, all the gods assembled at the temple of Marduk to pass judgment on man and to decide his fate during the coming year.

Likewise, the early Talmudists wrote that on Rosh Hashanah three books are opened in heaven: the Book of Life, listing those who have never sinned and who will be granted another year of life automatically; the Book of Death, in which are found the names of those who had committed many sins, who are condemned to die during the coming year; and a sort of in-between book listing those who are neither perfectly blameless nor grievously sinful—in other words, almost everyone. The fate of these latter individuals is held in abeyance for ten days, until Yom Kippur, when G-d will decide whether their repentance has earned them another year of life or whether they, too, shall die during the new year.

Therefore these ten Days of Awe are a time of prayer and penitence, and the ghettoites of Orsha took them very seriously; for they knew that at the end of those days G-d himself would look into their very souls and decide what fate should be meted to them on Yom Kippur. And during those ten days, any bad omen, no matter how trivial, was cause for great concern. So when several children and even a few adults came down with diphtheria, many feared that the end was not far behind.

Dr. Shatsky was the ghetto physician in those days, and a very able physician he was. He had studied medicine at a prestigious university in Germany, and while many of the less-educated doctors of the day still practiced leeching, cupping, and blood-letting, Dr. Shatsky was familiar with the latest techniques of surgery and the revolutionary theories of Louis Pasteur. When he realized that diphtheria had entered the ghetto he was prepared. He prescribed bedrest and liquids to help his patients convalesce, and tea of birch bark, which he knew contained the essential ingredient of aspirin, to reduce fever. He also knew the importance of public hygiene, and whereas most of the ghettoites thought that the disease was inflicted by divine decree, he knew that it was spread by bacteria, and so he wisely quarantined those who had become infected.

Thanks to Dr. Shatsky's enlightened ministrations, the spread of the epidemic was contained, and by the end of the Days of Awe most of the afflicted ghettoites were recovering nicely—all, that is, except poor Rosichka, the eight-year-old daughter of Gitella Justakovitch. This beautiful little girl was certainly the purest, most innocent child in all Orsha; the very thought of sin seemed never to have entered her curly-haired little head. The gossiping ghettoites couldn't imagine what secret sin she might have committed to incur the wrath of her creator. Nevertheless, the cruelest of fates seemed to have dogged her in recent days. Only six months earlier her father had been killed when his horse had spooked at a loud noise and bolted, throwing him from the wagon in which he was riding and breaking his neck. He died on the spot, and Rosichka and her mother were left with no income to sustain them, and throughout the period of mourning they had been supported by the generosity of their neighbors.

But still the angel of misfortune was not satisfied. No sooner had Rosichka and her mother thrown off their black mourning attire than the girl fell ill, and now she was suffering from the most severe symptoms and complications of diphtheria. It didn't seem fair, but there was no denying that the little girl was at death's door. Her face, formerly radiant, had become pale and drawn, and her beautiful bright brown eyes had grown dull. Her temperature had soared alarmingly, and she was profusely sweating away precious liquids, while her throat had become so badly swollen that she could barely swallow even the fluids Dr. Shatsky prescribed.

It was this last symptom that really worried Dr. Shatsky most. He was concerned that if the diphtheritic membrane continued to close off her windpipe, it might obstruct her breathing. Without an emergency tracheotomy, it would almost certainly result in the poor girl's death. This complication would be unusually severe, but as the disease progressed in Rosichka it seemed ever more likely, and so Dr. Shatsky decided to spend nights at Rosichka's bedside, ready to intervene the moment it became necessary.

On the seventh night of the Days of Awe, Dr. Shatsky was dozing fitfully on the uncomfortable cot Gitella had put out for him in Rosichka's room, haunted by the premonition that something would go awry during the night. At two o'clock in the morning he awakened with a start. What was that? A gasp? A groan? But he heard nothing—not even the labored sound of the sick girl's breathing. Had G-d really called the child to judgment?

The doctor was out of bed instantly, rushing to his patient's side. Rosichka was trying desperately to breath, but her trachea had become almost completely closed, choking the poor girl. Death seemed near.

Dr. Shatsky had already planned for this crisis, and did not hesitate. At the university in Germany he had performed many practice tracheotomies, first on cadavers and later on real patients, and that's what he did now. In almost no time at all he gave her a whiff of chloroform, a precious commodity in those days and reserved for the most serious of cases, and dexterously opened little Rosichka's windpipe. He ran a tube down into it to allow air to bypass her membranous trachea, then stepped back and offered a prayer to the All-Merciful to spare this innocent life.

To the doctor's great relief, the girl immediately began to breathe more freely. Her face relaxed and slowly turned from the fierce purple of the moribund back to the sallow pallor of the merely infirm. Her struggle ceased, and the anesthetic carried her into a deep, peaceful slumber. Dr. Shatsky dropped onto his cot with a heavy sigh and gave a silent prayer of thanks, then dropped off to sleep himself.

From that moment, Rosichka began to improve. Her body slowly but surely conquered the infection, and her dull eyes began to shine again. In a few days she was able to take liquids again, and the doctor gave her all the diluted warm milk and sugared water she could swallow. After several days he removed the tracheotomy tube, and Rosichka seemed well on the road to full recovery.

After four days at Rosichka's bedside, Dr. Shatsky finally returned home, grateful that a tragedy had been averted. Thanks to his efforts, only one elderly woman was lost to the diphtheria epidemic that year, but it could have been much worse. As the ten Days of Awe came to an end and Yom Kippur arrived, Dr. Shatsky and the rest of the ghettoites gave thanks to G-d—blessed be his holy name!—for allowing their families to enjoy another year on earth.

The Gypsy Wedding

IT WAS SPRINGTIME in the ghetto, and as bright and crisp and beautiful as springtime anywhere. In Orsha, as everywhere else, the Jewish people were celebrating Shevuoth. Shevuoth celebrates the covenant between G-d and the Jewish people, and commemorates the giving of the holy Torah on Mount Sinai many many, years ago, and for this reason it is also a time for young boys and girls to be confirmed as members of the Jewish faith. It is also a celebration of the first early harvests of spring, and the shul was decorated with fresh greens and offerings of all kinds of fruits. The ghetto women had brought trays and trays full of latkes made with cheeses and served with homemade apple sauce. Rabbi Shmul gave a sermon emphasizing the richness and fullness of nature, of Judaism, and of G-d—blessed be his name!—and stressed that at this fruitful time of year helping the needy was the greatest of all possible mitzvahs. It had indeed been a beautiful celebration, and now he and Helga had returned home overflowing with happiness and stuffed with latkes.

The rabbi had just thrown himself into a big, overstuffed chair and was about to nod off, when there came a knock at the door. Helga went to answer it, and both were surprised to see a rather garishly dressed and somewhat disheveled man and woman standing in the doorway. The man, who looked to be about forty, wore a vest that looked like it might once have been embroidered, a red shirt that must once have been very bright but whose high collar and wide cuffs were now badly soiled and frayed, and a pair of trousers that had probably always been a dull grayish brown. The woman with him was barely more than a girl. She wore a long, wide skirt of colorful patchwork and a shiny green silk blouse with billowing sleeves, and her wrists and ankles clattered with bangles as Helga ushered the two of them into the room.

It was easy to see they were Gypsies. Both of them had dark olive skin and long raven hair, and the man sported a bushy moustache and several days' worth of heavy stubble. Their eyes, too, were dark, like toasted chestnuts, but they held a bright, friendly gleam. The young woman's face was especially intriguing, for her long dark hair was set with wild goldenrod and asters, adding lustrous beauty to her full red lips and brilliant white teeth; but her features betrayed some vague anxiety, like a confused wild animal that has wandered into a village.

Shmul and Helga had heard of Gypsies, of course. In fact, they had heard quite a lot about them, although they had never actually met any. Just a few weeks ago they had heard a rumor that a band of Gypsies had made camp just outside a neighboring village, but the rabbi knew from professional experience to regard ghetto gossip with circumspection. There were very few Gypsies in the plains of Russia, because the nomadic bands preferred the warm southern climates of Italy and the rolling countryside of the Balkans. But the Rabbi and his wife, who always enjoyed learning about the customs of other people, knew that there were a few Gypsy families in their area, and perhaps hundreds more roaming throughout the land according to the seasons, raising horses, sheep, and goats, spinning wool and yarn, and gathering nuts and fruits to supplement the milk, meat, and cheese they produced. They were reputed to be more skillful horsemen than the Cossacks, to possess a deeper knowledge of herbs than the Chinese; and everyone knew they were masters of the fiddle and tambourine. It was even said that Gypsy women could see into the future by reading cards and tea leaves. But they had no written language or literature of any kind, for they were entirely ignorant of reading and writing. They had no permanent houses, no official nationality, no land they claimed as their own, nor any centralized government. For hundreds of years they had traveled wherever they pleased in brightly painted caravans and lived off the land, adopting the religion, customs, and language of whatever country they were sojourning in at the time.

This romantic life-style had always seemed very appealing to Shmul and Helga, especially during the frost-bound Orsha winters when there seemed to be nothing but cold, hunger, and tsouris in the ghetto, or when the Russian tax assessors came to collect, or, worse, when the Cossacks made one of their periodic wanton raids. In fact, it seemed a pretty good life most of the time. But they had also heard occasionally that Gypsies were thieves, kidnappers, and incestuous bands of momsers; that they hardly ever bathed; and that they performed lascivious dances around their campfires under the full moon.

The couple at the door certainly did not look like scoundrels, but it was obvious that they had come from somewhere very far away. In any case, Shmul and Helga welcomed them, and Helga prepared tea as always—although this time she didn't use the good china—and the Rabbi and the Gypsy couple sat down together at the table.

"You are the rebel of this village, no?" asked the man. He spoke only a little Russian, and he had such a thick accent Shmul could barely understand him.

"I am the rabbi," Shmul said, guessing his meaning. "My name is Shmul ben Shlomo; you can call me Shmul."

"Yes, thank you, Rebel Shmooze," said the man. "My name is Romero, and this is Marrina. We are Gypsies, and our camp is just a few kilometers from here. We have come to ask a favor of you. Can you marry us?"

Shmul was flabbergasted. Gypsies coming to a rabbi to be married? He hadn't learned anything about that in his years at the seminary. Surely the Gypsies had their own arrangements for marriage?

"Please excuse us, Rabbit," interrupted Marrina, who spoke slightly better Russian. "Normally we would go to our king to be married. Every Gypsy camp has a king, and marrying is one of his most important duties. But our king, Haslam is his name, is very sick. He hasn't left his tent in many weeks, and he is barely aware of the world around him. He gave us his blessing to be married, but he can't do it himself now. Probably he will die soon," she added, and Shmul was amazed to hear not a hint of sorrow in her voice. "So we come to you because the people told us you are the king of this village, and that you can marry people. Is this true, Rabbit Spool?"

Shmul was at a loss. He felt sorry for people who were about to lose their king, even if they weren't sorry themselves, and he wanted to help them if he could. To stall for time he asked, "Do your parents know you want to get married?"

"We have no parents," the young woman said, smiling. "Romero's parents died many, many years ago. My parents were killed by the Cossacks when I was very young. In fact, our king ordered Romero and his first wife, Luisa, to become my new father and mother, and they raised me from a baby. But during the winter Luisa got very sick, and now she's dead too. So now Romero and I have only each other; he needs a wife, and I need a husband. So you will marry us, King Rabbit Stool?"

"Just a minute," protested my great-great-grand-father. "First of all, I am not the king. This village has no king; it is part of the empire of the czar of Russia. And I am not a rabbit, I am a rabbi," he said carefully. "Rabbi Shmul. Do you know what a rabbi is? He is like a priest for Jewish people. Yes, I can marry people, but I marry them in the Jewish tradition; you, on the other hand, are not Jewish. Do you really want a Jewish wedding?"

"Yes, yes," assented Romero eagerly. "Jewish wedding. Is no different to us what religion. Jewish, okay—we become Jewish, and you marry us! Okay, Rabble Shul?"

"Well, you don't really have to be Jewish; it's just that the Jewish ceremony is the one I know. But how can you two be married? He is your foster fa-ther; she is your adoptive daughter. Don't Gypsies have rules about this sort of thing?"

"Rules?" said Romero. "Yes, rules. We do not marry our brother or sister, or mother or natural father. But Marrina and I are not really related—only live together. So we know we can be a family, no? And our king told us rules was okay, we can get married. So you marry us? Now, today?"

Shmul tried to think. True, the couple were not really related by blood, but their age difference was huge. And true, they did not really have to be Jewish in order to be married by him in the eyes of G-d—much less so in the eyes of the Russian government. But it wasn't as simple as that. Could such a marriage be held in the shul? And what about the ketubah (nuptial agreement), and what about the chuppa? Shmul wanted to help them— had he himself not said at the service this very morning that to help the poor was the greatest mitzvah of all? But he needed time to think.

"No, I'm sorry," he said. "Maybe I can marry you, but not today." The couple looked crestfallen, and Shmul hastily continued. "But perhaps tomorrow. There are certain preparations that must be made. I must ask the shames—he is the man who runs the shul, the building where our weddings take place. And we must have witnesses to the wedding in order to make it legal. So here is what you must do. Go back to your camp and return here tomorrow with a few friends or relatives who may serve as witnesses. Meanwhile I will think this over and make whatever arrangements are needed. If all goes well—*if* all goes well—you can be married then."

Romero and Marrina brightened at this, but they still seemed troubled and seemed not to understand the difficult issues they had raised for the rabbi. Looking hopeful but dubious, they took their leave, promising to return the next day.

"Thank you, Rubber Shmooze," said Romero. "We

come back tomorrow. But we must be married soon. As soon as the king is dead, our camp will move, and then what will we do? So we will see you to-morrow, to be married."

When the couple had gone, Shmul turned to Helga, his eyebrows arched almost to the brim of his yarmulke. He was stumped.

"Whatever am I to do?" he asked her. "I've never married a non-Jewish couple before; my father never did, and I've never heard of anyone doing it. I've certainly never had any dealings with Gypsies; I have no idea what their own marriage customs are or what they really expect of me."

"Nanu," said Helga, putting her arm around his shoulder. "Come sit down and finish the tea, and let's talk."

They sat down facing each other, and neither said anything for a moment. "They did seem like a nice young couple," offered Helga after she'd taken a quick inventory of the silverware on the table.

"Young? Why, he's old enough to be her father—in fact, he almost is her father!"

"Well, she is a bit young, but I think she's old enough to know her own mind. And they certainly know one another well enough. Anyway, he's not really her father at all; just a stranger who's been kind enough to give her a home and a family. And if their king has already given his blessing, then there is nothing to prevent their marriage at all, at least not by their own customs."

Shmul had to admit that what his wife said made sense. There really was no reason the couple should not be married. "But why couldn't they wait for their king to recover, or to be replaced? Don't Gypsies even have a shadchen? And why come to a rabbi in a little ghetto like this? Why not get a civil wedding in Smolensk? Why couldn't they at least have gone to Father Pietr? Why me?"

"Nu," said his wife after a pause. "They couldn't get a civil wedding because the authorities would certainly arrest them for something or other. They couldn't go to Father Pietr because he can only marry Orthodox Christians. It seems like they'd be willing enough to convert for the occasion, but to become a Catholic you have to go to catechism and take confirmation, and that takes time. No, you're the only one they *could* turn to. That's why you."

"As usual," said Shmul resignedly. "But I can always refuse. I could think of half a dozen good reasons not to perform the ceremony."

"And if you do? They'll just go the next rabbi in the next ghetto along their caravan route, and it will just be his problem instead of yours. Or else they won't get married at all; they'll just keep living together unwed, and their children will all be momsers. And didn't you say yourself only this morning that charity to the poor was the greatest of all mitzvahs? So what more poor people could you find?"

Once again, Shmul couldn't argue. It was his duty and his alone, he realized, to marry the couple as best he could.

"But what about the ceremony? Mustn't we have a ketubah? Can we do it in the shul? And what about a chuppa? And what about smashing the glass?"

"Nu, love, there I can't advise you," said the rebbitsin. "Better you should ask Shames Drayzuch what he thinks, and do as the two of you decide."

Of course she was right again. Shmul shrugged on his coat, pulled on his beaver hat, and set out to find the shames.

When the rabbi had finished giving Shames Drayzuch his desultory description of the affair at hand, he was astonished to see that the shames was elated.

"Wonderful!" exclaimed Drayzuch. "I thought the whole spring would go by without a wedding in our temple." He always called the shul "our temple," even though to everyone else it was just a shul. "Jews or not, a wedding is a wedding. And this will be extra special—Gypsies, right here in our temple!"

Rabbi Shmul was still not convinced. "But we haven't time to make a ketubah. How can they be married without a ketubah?"

"However they make an agreement in Gypsy-dom, I'm sure that will be fine," said the shames. "Anyway, if they weren't serious about getting married, why would they bother to come to us at all?"

"Well, it has to be a Jewish wedding," insisted the Rabbi. "And the prayers will have to be in He-brew, and the Gypsies won't understand them."

"Yes, but the prayers are to G-d, not to them. Maybe you could explain them a little bit first," suggested Drayzuch.

"Well, I suppose so. But the men will have to wear yarmulkes, of course, if it's to be a wedding in the presence of G-d."

"Of course, of course," said the shames. "And we'll have to bring out the chuppa, too, and decorations."

"Okay, okay," agreed Shmul. "But let's not smash the glass. They won't understand that it symbolizes the destruction of the temple, and they're likely to think it's an invitation to start partying and smashing things up."

Just then the shames's wife, Chupa-Ala, entered and overheard the conversation. "A wedding?" she squealed. "In our temple? Such a mitzvah! And Gypsies? Oh, dear, I'll have to bring something to celebrate—of course! I can bring the leftover latkes from this morning! Oh, Yussel—oh, Rabbi—it will be wonderful!"

The thing seemed settled, and my great-great-grandfather was at last convinced that every possible objection he could think of to this unorthodox wedding of Gypsies in the ghetto had been answered. He went home and told Helga they were all set.

❧

Early the next morning the Gypsies returned to Grandpa's house, attired as before and accompanied by three rather rough-looking men who were clearly anxious for the fun to start. They were to be the witnesses, apparently, although it seemed they understood almost no Russian at all. But before they left for the shul, Shmul addressed them all in earnest.

"You understand that this is to be a Jewish wedding?"

"Yes," said Marrina.

"Yes," said Romero. "We Jewish now, go get married."

"That's not at all necessary," said the rabbi. "We'll marry you just as you are." Then he described the streamlined ceremony he and the shames had planned, and told them what the prayers would say. "But you must wear these at the ceremony," he added, producing four black yarmulkes. The men removed their battered woolen hats and tried on the yarmulkes, and they laughed at each other and shouted in a language the rabbi could not understand. But they caught his serious mien and fell in behind him as he and Helga led them to the shul.

The shames and his wife were waiting outside the shul, and all nine of them—four Jews and five Gypsies—filed into the shul together. The Gypsies, who had apparently never been in any kind of temple before, seemed impressed and spoke in hushed tones. Two of the witnesses tried to doff their yarmulkes out of respect, but Helga gently restrained them. They looked in amazement at the spare but dignified furnishings of the shul and especially at the chuppa, and one of them told Helga in an awestruck whisper that this was the first time any of their band had been married indoors.

Before the ceremony began, Rabbi Shmul produced a simple document he had written the night before stating that Romero and Marrina were legally married on this day. The shames signed it with glee, and the two lovers and the three witnesses each put their "x" at the bottom. Then Rabbi Shmul and Shames Drayzuch went up to the lectern and began the prayers. At first the entire party stood solemnly with their heads bowed, but as the rabbi went on it became apparent that none of the wedding party understood anything of what was being said. The witnesses were distractedly looking about the room, and before Shmul finished reading, they had wandered off to various corners of the shul and were busily examining the furnishings—inspecting the design of the benches and chairs and marveling at the fittings of the doors and windows as though they had never seen such things in all their lives. One of the men had found the holy ark on the bima, and after admiring the tapestry covering he pushed it aside, opened its doors, and began running his fingers over the silver shields that covered the Torahs. This made the shames very nervous, and he elbowed the rabbi to hurry him along. Shmul skipped to the end, and when he closed the prayer book and addressed Romero and Marrina to administer the vows, all the witnesses immediately dropped their investigations and hastily reassembled before him.

"Romero, Miss Marrina," he said with a sigh of relief, "you are now husband and wife."

The Gypsies exploded into cheers. The witnesses

slapped both the bride and groom hard on the back, and everyone, even the rabbi, embraced. Chupa-Ala and Helga brought out a table and arranged some chairs, and spread out the latkes and tea, and the entire party sat down to the little feast. The Gypsies had never eaten latkes before, and for the witnesses this was the highlight of the entire day. They stuffed themselves and laughed with their mouths full until every last crumb of crust was gone.

As the wedding party took their leave, the four ghettoites stood in the doorway and waved goodbye. "Thank you, thank you, Rubber Boot!" effused Romero, and Marrina gave Shmul and Helga a warm embrace. "Tonight, our camp, very big celebrate," said Romero. "Big bonfire, much music and dance. Much arak, too! You will come, please?" Fortunately, though, he did not show any great disappointment when the ghettoites politely declined, remembering among other things that the food would not be kosher. So the Gypsies departed for their camp as boisterously happy as a band of children, and Helga and Shmul exchanged a warm smile, glad they had taken a chance on such simple and grateful people.

It was not until the next evening, a Friday, that it was discovered that the silver shield was missing from one of the shul's Torahs. The shames and the rabbi were holding the usual shabbes service, and when they opened the ark for the Torah reading and saw that one of the scrolls lay naked and exposed, their jaws dropped to their knees. The shames skillfully pretended to remove the shield as he withdrew the scroll, so that the congregation wouldn't know that anything was wrong; but as his eyes met the rabbi's they both knew instantly what had happened: the Gypsies had taken one of the silver shields.

After the service they conferred in private in the back room of the shul. They had grown so fond of Romero and Marrina and had become so friendly with their witnesses during the wedding reception that they could scarcely believe what was now all too plain. They remembered the Gypsy men wandering about the shul during yesterday's wedding, and the shames got a sick feeling when he recalled the man fingering the embossed writing on the shield.

Then it was the rabbi's turn to feel his stomach sink, for he recalled that Romero and Marrina had been in such a hurry to be married because their caravan was about to leave very soon. Maybe they were gone already, and with them any hope of recovering the Torah shield.

Nevertheless, Rabbi Shmul and Shames Drayzuch decided to drive out to where the Gypsy camp was supposed to be and investigate. And although they were desperate to recover the shield, both of them still hoped they wouldn't find it among their new friends.

They waited impatiently all day Saturday, for they couldn't travel on the shabbes; then, very early

Sunday morning, the shames brought his carriage to the rabbi's house to pick him up, and they set off. Before long they saw the smoke of the Gypsies' fires, and as they approached they saw that they were just in time. The Gypsies were already preparing to move out. But as they rode into the outskirts of the camp, a man came running up to greet them. It was Romero.

"Rebel Shmooze! Rebel Shmooze! We are so happy to have you in our camp. Please, come into our tent. Marrina will like to see you, and...and I have something to give you."

Another Gypsy came up and took the reins of the shames's horse while Shmul and Drayzuch climbed down and followed Romero to a tent near the center of the camp, one of the few tents still not packed away. Romero held open the flap for them to duck and enter. Inside, Marrina sat folding old clothes and tying them into a bundle. And there on a low pallet was the missing silver shield.

"Rebel, I am very sorry," stammered Romero, handing the shield to Shmul, who passed it to Shames Drayzuch, "but one of our friends take this by accident from your temple during our wedding. Oh, Rebel, such a beautiful wedding! But our friend was look around and he find a closet, and when he open the door he saw two fancy dressed-up bundles. He don't know what they are, but they are very beautiful. And then he saw this silver around them, and he take one off to see what it is. We have seen the silver of the Turks, but we have never seen something like this. Then suddenly you called him to hear our wedding. He was confused, he don't want to slow the wedding, and he thought you maybe mad, so he hide the thing under his coat. When we go—well, he forget to give it back.

"Rebel, he didn't mean no harm. People say Gypsies are thieves, but it's not true, Rebel. We are only very curious about your strange customs and your beautiful decorations. We only want to see and know. So we went together yesterday to your village to return your beautiful decoration. But when we get to the temple, many many people there. We don't know what to do, so we come home. We plan to visit your village again on our way today. But now you come to our camp instead! How wonderful! Now you have your decoration, and I have my wife, and everyone is happy. No, Rebel Shmooze?"

Indeed, everyone was, not least Rabbi Shmul and Shames Drayzuch, who were relieved that the faith they had placed in their new friends and the trust they had shown by marrying them in the shul had not been a mistake. They sat down together and Marrina served tea and some kind of Gypsy pastry, which was very delicious, and they drank a toast with the tea to the newlyweds.

Then Shmul explained to Romero, who translated for the several curious visitors who had meanwhile come into the tent, what a Torah was and what its shield meant. One of the men, the witness who had taken the shield, asked Romero a question.

"Friend want to know, what is magical writing on this shield?"

Shmul explained that these were the names of the twelve tribes of the Jewish people, and when Romero repeated it to the other Gypsies a gasp of awe went up.

"Tribes?" asked Romero incredulously. "Your people travel also in tribes? Oh, Rebel, I knew you were our friends. You are tribal people, just like Gypsies! Yes, Rebel, I knew we can trust you, and now I know our marriage will be happy forever, because you are really our family too!"

Everyone smiled at this revelation, and they all lifted their teacups in a toast of friendship between the Gypsies and the Jews.

"And who knows," said Romero after they drank. "Maybe someday your people will wander in the countryside like us. Maybe someday you will know how it is to have other people call you bad names. And then maybe you will know how grateful we Gypsy people are to you for giving us our beautiful wedding and being our good Jewish friends!"

Maybe someday we will, thought my great-great-grandfather ironically as he raised his glass yet again. Maybe we will.

The Curse of Mikalo's Hollow

AT ONE TIME there were vast forests covering the entire landscape of low hills and valleys where the town of Orsha now lies. Climatologists and archeologists tell us that the area was once a tropical jungle bristling with cycads, palms, and primitive conifers. Early traders and explorers who passed through the territory, including Mencius and Marco Polo, wrote of large, dark forests of firs, beeches, and maples.

But all that was long, long ago. By my great-great-grandfather's time, nearly all of the land had been cleared to make way for the wheat and dairy farms that even today are the chief industry of the region. Near Orsha there remained but a single small forest whose few trees supplied the modest needs of the town, and this, too, would have been chopped down for lumber and firewood, if the wood hadn't been too expensive for most people to buy. For people of that day had no love of wilderness, as we do today. To them it represented the wild, the chaotic, and the pagan. The forest near Orsha was known to local residents as the Enchanted Forest, and the superstitious townsfolk knew it to be not only infested with wolves and bears, but also inhabited by wicked witches and pugnacious elves who would capture and enslave any humans who wandered unwarily into their territory. They were terrified of the forest, and their very fear kept them from discovering how baseless that fear really was.

Not everyone was so afraid, however. For there lived in the ghetto a woodcutter named Yonkel ben Kassala, a tall, broad-shouldered, muscular man who went into the Enchanted Forest every fall to harvest firewood. Reb Yonkel was afraid of nothing, and went alone into the forest without a care. When the ghettoites watched him disappear among the trees, they were certain he'd never come out alive. But after a week or more of camping among the wolves, bears, witches, and elves, he'd come back out again whistling merrily, his wagon loaded with freshly cut logs, and his tongue overflowing with incredible stories of his adventures.

For Reb Yonkel was also known all over Orsha as a teller of tall tales. As he worked in the forest he kept his mind busy inventing the yarns with which he would regale his friends all winter long—how he'd fought off wolves that had surrounded his campfire, or how he'd chased a bear that had jumped up on his wagon, stolen a five-meter tree trunk, and made off with it over the hills. And of course Yonkel's fantastic tales didn't help the ghettoites overcome their fear of the wilderness, but only reinforced their superstitions.

It was just after the Tisha b'Av holiday, the "Holiday of Mourning" for the destruction of the temple in Jerusalem, that Reb Yonkel the woodcutter appeared at my great-great-grandfather's door in a state of extreme agitation. Rabbi Shmul had never seen him like this before: the huge, burly man was pale as a sheet, his eyes dilated in terror, and he was obviously shaken to his bones. Grandpa invited him inside and sat him down at the table while Helga fetched the tea and mandelbrot, but at first the woodcutter could not even speak.

"Yonkel, Yonkel," pleaded Grandpa, "calm yourself and tell me what the trouble is."

Helga set down the tea tray and poured a glass of tea for the woodcutter, but his hands shook so hard he splashed it all over the table.

"Rabbi, help me," he gasped. "I've had the most dreadful experience. I can hardly believe it myself, but I swear to you, this is not just another woodcutter's tall tale. It's all true, Rabbi, every word, and if you don't help me I'll be dead before the shabbes."

"Slow down, slow down," said Rabbi Shmul. "Take your time and tell me all about it." He couldn't imagine what might have upset this fearless man so much.

The woodcutter took a deep breath and began. "I've just returned from the Enchanted Forest, where I was cutting wood as usual. Everything was fine until just yesterday, and now my life is in jeopardy. You know how the villagers say the forest is haunted; I never believed it before, but, Rabbi, it's true!

"Two days ago I finished cutting wood up by Gronliki Hill, and my wagon was almost full of fine, big logs. But I still had room for a couple more, so on my way back I stopped at the place they call Mikalo's Hollow." As he said the name, his hands started trembling again. "I'm not a superstitious man, Rabbi, but I never liked that place. The trees grow so thick there that sunlight never reaches the ground. It's always dark and cold and damp, and frankly even I find it kind of spooky.

"Well, as soon I got there I started getting the creeps, and the hair on my arms started to stand on end. But I said to myself, "Oh, come off it, Yonkel, you old fool. It's just a forest full of trees, and that only means more work for you. Get busy and let's clear some space to get some light in here.'

"So I got out my ax and found a magnificent tree just waiting to be felled. It must have been a very old tree—its trunk was almost a whole meter across, and it was covered with moss. Good, I thought, I can fill my wagon with just this one more tree. So I started chopping. The wood was hard as iron, and I had to stop several times to sharpen my blade. It was tough work, but I didn't mind, because I knew the log would fetch a good price once it was cleaned up. It took nearly the whole morning to cut the uphill side, and almost all afternoon to cut the downhill side, but still the tree didn't fall. I've never seen anything like it. This tree has a will to live, I thought to myself. But finally, after I'd cut almost all the way through it, it started to go. What was left of the trunk splintered apart with a horrible ripping sound, and then the boughs started to sway. It was such a huge tree it kept falling and falling and falling, and when it finally hit the ground it made the most terrific crash I've ever heard, and branches and needles and splinters of wood went flying in every direction.

"After the crash the forest seemed still as death, and I stood staring at the stump, amazed at how big it was. That's when it happened. Right before my eyes, the stump started to shake in the ground, and a little man popped up right out of the wood! I couldn't believe my eyes, but there he was: no more than half a meter tall, dressed in skins and furs, hopping up and down on the stump and cursing me in the vilest language I've ever heard in my life.

"'Look what you've done, foolish man!' he shouted. 'You've cut down my house. This is where I live, where I've lived for hundreds and hundreds of years while your ignorant people have come and gone. Now you've come here without permission and cut down my house, and now I have no home!

"'This is my curse on you, you stupid man: You must plant another tree for me immediately, so that I will have a place to live. It must be at least ten years old, and you must plant it within five meters of this spot. I will give you four days—and four days only—and if you do not do exactly as I command, you will die!'

"What am I to do, Rabbi? I can't plant such a large tree all by myself, and I can't get anyone to go into the Enchanted Forest to help me. Two days have passed already, and time is running out."

Reb Yonkel was now shaking uncontrollably, and his voice was choked off so that he could speak no more. After a moment he actually began to cry.

Rabbi Shmul was dumbfounded. He'd heard the stories of vicious elves in the woods, but he'd never believed them. He'd also heard plenty of Reb Yonkel's meshuggeneh stories, and never believed them, either. But there was no denying the fear that had gripped this once-fearless man, and it was obvious that Yonkel himself, at least, believed every word he had spoken.

Still, Grandpa had his doubts. He'd seen people before whose fear had overtaken their reason and who had actually begun to believe their own wild stories. Shmulke the yenta often grew to believe the "stretchers" that were her stock in trade. Maybe, he thought, Reb Yonkel had gotten himself so worked up during a week alone in the woods that he was actually starting to see things. If so, all the rabbi had to do was go with him to the woods and try to dispel his irrational fears.

"Well," he said finally, "why don't I go with you and see if we can't talk some sense into this elf. I've dealt with plenty of angry people before, and an angry elf can't be much different. Do you think it would help?"

The woodcutter was extremely grateful and more than a little relieved. He and my great-great-grandfather set out that very afternoon for the Enchanted Forest. It wasn't far, and soon they arrived at Mikalo's Hollow. It was indeed a spooky place. Long boughs festooned with tatters of moss reached out over the road like grasping fingers, and from somewhere the stench of a stagnant spring tinged the cold, damp air. In a dense grove lay the tree the woodcutter had felled the day before, just as he had left it, a fallen giant. But the little elf, if he existed, was nowhere to be seen.

"Mister Elf!" called Yonkel. "Mister Elf, come out! We've come to talk to you!" But there was no reply.

"Well," said Rabbi Shmul. "It looks like your elf has found himself a new home already. I guess the curse is off."

"I suppose so," said Reb Yonkel as he looked around nervously. He called a few times more, but when there was no response Rabbi Shmul convinced him to give it up and go home, for the sun was already about to set.

But the next day, when Yonkel returned to clean up the felled tree and bring it home, there was the wicked little elf again, sitting on the tree stump, madder than ever.

"Who was that man you brought here yesterday," he screamed, "and why did you bring him here? And why have you not planted a tree as I commanded?"

"He's our rabbi," answered the woodcutter, shaking in his boots, "and I brought him to talk to you. I can't plant your tree myself, and no one will come to the forest to help me."

"Well, you'd better find someone fast," insisted the elf. "You've got just one day left, and then *k-k-k-k-k-k!*" He drew a finger across his throat, and his meaning was all too clear.

"Yessir, Mr. Elf, I promise!" Reb Yonkel said, and with that he jumped back up on his wagon and rushed back to the ghetto. He went straight to the rabbi's house, told him what had happened, and insisted that the rabbi come help him plant the tree. Rabbi Shmul tried again to calm him, but Reb Yonkel would not be dissuaded. Oh well, thought the rabbi, if that's what it takes for him to get over this, that's what we'll have to do.

Together they went around to the other houses and gathered half a dozen men with picks and shovels. "Please come help us," pleaded Reb Yonkel. "We're just going to plant a tree, and we'll be back by sunset." He didn't dare tell them the whole story. The ghettoites were suspicious when they saw how agitated he was, and they couldn't understand why a man who made his living cutting trees suddenly wanted to plant one. But when they saw that the rabbi was already seated in the wagon they agreed to come along.

By the time they got to the Enchanted Forest, Reb Yonkel's rising fear had become obvious, and the men all looked around nervously as they drove beneath the tall trees to Mikalo's Hollow. The stump and the log were still there, of course, but there was no sign of the elf.

The ghettoites climbed down from the wagon warily, and in teams of two they began looking for a tree to transplant. In the thick of the woods not far away they found a tree that had been uprooted by a severe windstorm a few weeks before. Almost all of its roots were exposed, and if it were not replanted it would surely die soon. Yonkel said the tree looked good, so they brought the wagon up as close as they could, and together they hoisted the top of the tree aboard and shlepped it back to where the stump was. They dug a hole nearby—Reb Yonkel insisted it be not more than five meters from the stump— and using a system of ropes slung over the branches of other nearby trees, they hoisted it upright and mounded dirt over its roots.

Reb Yonkel urged the men on and shoveled like mad, and didn't relax until the tree was planted. When it was finally standing upright in its new location, he at last allowed himself to stand back and rest, and the worry faded from his face. Okay, Mr. Elf, he thought, there's your new home.

Just at that moment there was a stirring in the trees above them. The men looked up and saw a black raven fly through the hollow and perch at the top of the tree they had just planted. It was enormous, even for a raven, and it looked even bigger as it sat on the limb and puffed out its feathers.

The bird looked down directly at Reb Yonkel and cocked its shining black eye at him. "Grawwwwk," it croaked in an ominous tone. Then it shook itself, raised its beak to the sky, and called out "Caw! Caw! Caw!" as if to announce its claim on the new tree. Then it disappeared into the foliage.

"Did you see that!" said Reb Yonkel, pointing. But the bird was already gone. "That was the elf I told you about. He turned himself into a raven— that must be how they travel! And," he added, turning to Rabbi Shmul, "he says his new tree is acceptable, and he will not kill me.

"Thank you, my friends, thank you! You have saved my life!"

Rabbi Shmul stared up into the tree. Could it be? Nonsense! There's no such things as elves, he thought to himself. This was just a bird claiming a new roost, nothing more, nothing less. The important thing was that Reb Yonkel, whatever he really believed, had done what needed to be done to relieve himself of the "curse," whether it was inflicted by an elf or by his own vivid imagination.

Still, as they all boarded the wagon and headed back to the ghetto, Rabbi Shmul didn't remind the woodcutter that he'd forgotten to take along his log, which probably lies in Mikalo's Hollow to this day.

The Royal Birth

IN THE SOCIAL HIERARCHY of old Russia, Jews occupied one of the lowest positions of all. Centuries ago they had moved east from Germany and central Europe, the land they called Ashkenaz, when tolerance of their religion and life-style began to wane in those lands, and they made new homes in the shtetls of Poland, Czechoslovakia, Hungary, Rumania, and Russia. In Russia they were permitted, "by the generosity of the czar," to live in the country, but were restricted to ghettos like the one on the outskirts of Orsha. The Jewish people as a class were greatly disdained by the Russians. When it came to rights, they had none; when it came to respect, they had even less, if that is possible. To

149

most Russians, Jews were a subhuman life form, tolerated mostly out of necessity.

Yet individual Jews were often treated well by individual Russians. Rabbi Shmul, for example, was very highly respected by most of the local Russians, and Father Pietr, the priest of Orsha's Russian Orthodox Christian church, often asked advice from him on thorny issues raised by his congregation. Reb Nachem, the ghetto baker, did almost as much business with town Russians as with ghetto Jews, for his strict adherence to the laws of koshreth gave his breads a quality that was known far and wide, whereas many of the Russian bakers would sell anything that wasn't green or moving. Likewise, Reb Nathan, the tailor, sewed clothes in a style his parents and grandparents had brought from Ashkenaz, and when that style became popular among Russians, there was nowhere else for them to find it but in the ghetto tailor shop. Thus, while Jews were mostly tolerated and ignored, most Russians would conveniently forget their prejudices when it suited their purposes. And this was true even of Czar Alexander himself.

One January during my great-great-grandfather's tenure as the rabbi of Orsha, a rumor spread that the czarina was with child. The news was greeted joyously by everyone, for it was well known that the royal family was as yet without issue, and the throne of Russia was without an heir. To the Russians of Orsha it was a cause for celebration; to the neighboring Jews, who feared anything associated with the czar, it was just news, and nothing more. They never imagined that the event would ever reach their ghetto the way it eventually did, for it was none other than the ghetto physician, Dr. Shatsky, who presided over the royal birth.

It came about in this way: When the czar learned that his wife had finally become pregnant he was overjoyed. At last he would have an heir—for in his vanity he was certain that the child would be a boy, although of course there was no way of knowing such a thing in those days. Immediately he began a search for the best physician he could find, and as soon as he consulted with his palace doctors he learned that one of the greatest physicians in the world was Professor Max Himmelsdorf, the head of the university medical school in Berlin—who also happened to be the mentor of Orsha's Dr. Shatsky. And so he wrote Professor Himmelsdorf as follows:

THE IMPERIAL PALACE OF THE RUSSIAN EMPIRE
MOSCOW

Esteemed Professor Himmelsdorf,
    By the grace of God, the czarina of Russia has become pregnant with the next heir to the imperial throne, who will be born in early March of this year. This is a momentous occasion in the history of the empire, and therefore in the history of the world, and it is of the utmost importance that every conceivable precaution and advantage be

taken to ensure that this divine gift be brought successfully to fruition.

It has come to our attention that your reputation as an obstetrician of international acclaim is well regarded by the members of your profession, who consider your ability second to none. Therefore we request your presence at Moscow as chief obstetrician in attendance upon the birth of the next czar of Russia, in order that we may be assured of an auspicious beginning to the career of the most wise and good leader of our country's future.

Although we may not command a citizen of a foreign country, we nevertheless hope that the continuous cordial relations between our empire and your country will further impress you with the import of this event, and that you will acquiesce to this imperial request.

Most cordially,

ALEXANDER II, CZAR OF THE RUSSIAN EMPIRE

Needless to say, Professor Himmelsdorf was impressed, not only by the bombast of the czar's epistle, but by the very flattering nature of the request. It was a commission no physician would willingly decline. Nevertheless, he felt he could not agree to go to Moscow, for it happened that his own wife was also expecting their first child at about the same time. But it occurred to him that there was an alternative very near at hand, and therefore he sent his regrets to Czar Alexander thus:

UNIVERSITY MEDICAL COLLEGE
BERLIN

Your Highness,

It is with great joy that I learn that her highness, the czarina, is expecting the birth of a child [the professor did not assume, as had the czar, that it would be a boy], and I am honored to receive your request that I attend the delivery. But I regret that it is impossible for me to accept your commission due to the pregnancy of my own wife with our firstborn.

If you highness will allow, however, I would like to suggest another physician of the highest competence, who, I am sure, will be pleased to attend the royal birth.

Dr. Yussel Shatsky was my pupil at Berlin University, and I can recommend him to you without reservation. Dr. Shatsky was certainly the very best student it has ever been my pleasure to instruct. Of particular pertinence, Dr. Shatsky excelled above all in the field of obstetrics and gynecology.

Dr. Shatsky now resides in the small town of Orsha, which is only a day's journey from Moscow by train, and thus he can be available to you even more conveniently than myself. And you have my assurance that you may rely upon him with every confidence.

Sincerely,

PROFESSOR M. HIMMELSDORF

The professor never mentioned that Dr. Shatsky was a Jew; indeed, he barely thought about it. Yussel Shatsky was an excellent doctor, and would have been so even if he were a cannibal. Professor Himmelsdorf thought no more about it, but made a copy of his letter to the czar and sent it, along with the czar's original letter, to Dr. Shatsky in Orsha, telling him he might expect a summons from Moscow soon.

Dr. Shatsky was stunned when he received the news. He'd heard of the czarina's pregnancy, of course, but he had never even considered that he, a humble ghetto doctor, would have anything at all to do with it. At first he was flattered that his old mentor remembered him so kindly; then he was elated to think that he might actually receive an imperial commission. But then a sudden dread fell over him: what if the czar should summon him to Moscow and then discover he was a Jew? He would certainly be humiliated—he might even be executed. Of course, neither Dr. Shatsky nor anyone else knew what the czar's attitude toward Jews might be. But was not the czar the ruler of the country that had relegated the Jewish people to the ghettos? Was he not commander in chief of the Cossacks, whose wanton raids were responsible for the slaughter of so many of his fellow ghettoites? Surely the czar must know of the great oppression of the Jews; and if he knew of it, didn't that mean he also condoned it, perhaps even ordered it himself? For the next week Dr. Shatsky lived in fear of the knock on the door he hoped would never come.

A few weeks later, however, the knock did come, and when Dr. Shatsky answered he was amazed to see a very well-dressed Russian who introduced himself cordially as Count Vernichik and informed him politely that the czar commanded his presence in Moscow the next day to attend the royal birth. The doctor was taken by surprise, for the professor's letter and the czar's had said that the birth would not occur until March, and it was still only January. But here was the count already, and his carriage, a fine black phaeton, waited before the house, a liveried chauffeur ready at the reins. The count suggested they could leave immediately, if the doctor were agreeable. Of course, Dr. Shatsky knew that it was a command, not a request, but he was somewhat reassured by the count's deferential manner. Still, as he excused himself to pack his things, he wondered if he was not going to meet his doom.

Dr. Shatsky packed a small bag with a few changes of clothes, not knowing how long he might be gone, or when, if ever, he would return. He thought he should take his bag of surgical instruments, but as he looked inside he realized that his simple tools of wood, metal, and ivory would probably be unworthy of his royal patient. Nevertheless, he decided to bring along the special obstetrical forceps that Professor Himmelsdorf had given him when he passed his final examination. These were the latest advance in obstetrical instruments at the time. They had long been the family secret of John and William Hunter of London, but when knowledge of their use was finally disclosed to the world, they were quickly recognized for their unique usefulness in certain complicated situations, as for example when a tight fit between the baby and its mother's pelvis made unaided delivery difficult. It had become the custom at the university in Berlin to award a pair of silver obstetrical forceps to the leading graduate every year, and Dr. Shatsky took great pride in owning his. He was sure that the czar could procure any instrument he might ask for, with the one exception of modern forceps, and so he packed his own among his folded shirts and trousers. As he closed the bag with its frayed leather strap, he felt a sudden twinge of fear at what might happen to him, a common rural doctor and a Jew, if there should be a problem with the royal birth. He hoped he would not have to use his prized forceps. And what if the birth were so difficult that he had to resort to a cesarean section? The usual result of so serious an operation was death of the mother or of the child—and most often of both. And what would become of him then? He paused to offer a prayer that all would go well; then he hefted his bag and returned to the waiting count.

Count Vernichik helped Dr. Shatsky into the carriage, and they rode off toward the train station. If the count noticed that they were driving through the rutted streets of a ghetto, he gave no sign of it; but the ghettoites certainly noticed the black phaeton with their doctor inside, and every window was full of peering faces.

When they arrived at the station they found the

czar's private train waiting for them, and a uniformed porter took Dr. Shatsky's luggage and helped them aboard. The train was like no train Dr. Shatsky had ever seen; in fact, he'd never even seen a house so sumptuously appointed. Behind the engine were three cars, each brightly painted in red with the imperial emblem in gold, and trimmed in expensive polished hardwood. The first car was a sitting room, furnished with armchairs and divans with embroidered upholstery, graceful Louis XIV side tables, and an ornately inlaid writing desk, all of which were emblazoned with the czar's imperial emblem. Its floor was covered with an elaborate Oriental carpet, its windows were hung with heavy draperies, and on its walls hung richly framed portraits of the royal family.

Next was the dining car, in the middle of which stood a huge round table covered with a gleaming white lace tablecloth. Although it seemed that only Dr. Shatsky and Count Vernichik were aboard, a dozen upholstered chairs were drawn up to the table, and it was set with a full complement of crystal stemware, painted china, and shining cutlery of real silver, including forks and spoons of several different sizes at each place.

At the end of the train, where the noise of the engine would be stifled by heavy draperies and carpets, was the bedroom car, with two huge beds separated by a curtain of exquisite and colorful brocade. The porter had already deposited Dr. Shatsky's suitcase at the foot of one of the beds, and the doctor was embarrassed to see how shabby it looked in these luxurious surroundings. To his relief, the count seemed not to notice.

The doctor and the count returned to the sitting room car, and a waiter in a starched white jacket brought them snifters of fine cognac as they conversed and watched the snowy hills roll by. The count seemed interested in medicine, although Dr. Shatsky noticed at once that what little he knew of it was out of date by nearly a century. The doctor eagerly told him of his studies in Berlin and of the new theories of Pasteur and Lister. The count listened politely and nodded, though he seemed not to understand. Dr. Shatsky tried to make the subject as interesting as he could and tried to steer the conversation away from politics and religion, for he still was not sure that the count knew he was Jewish, and his nerves remained on edge lest the dreaded subject be broached. Fortunately, however, it never came up, and finally the waiter reappeared and invited them to dinner.

The big round table in the dining car was now laid with silver platters and porcelain bowls heaped with the most exotic gourmet foods. Although he'd only heard of such things, Dr. Shatsky recognized roasted squabs, braised salmon, and entire wheels of cheeses imported from Holland, England, and France. Dr. Shatsky was overwhelmed. There was enough food here to feed an army, but only he and Count Vernichik to eat it! He was heartbroken to think that there was very little of it he could eat, anyway, for he assumed that none of it was kosher; but he nibbled at the sautéed vegetables, freshly baked bread, and delicious fruit compote, while Count Vernichik gorged himself on everything. The count's favorite delicacy of all, he said, was the savory smoked whitefish, procured exclusively for the imperial table from a special fish merchant in the village of Groski, and Dr. Shatsky couldn't resist trying a tender, tasty morsel. If they eat fish in heaven, he thought, no doubt they buy it in Groski!

An hour later the count was stuffed and Dr. Shatsky was finished nibbling, yet they had eaten barely a quarter of what was served. They repaired to the sitting room, where the waiter offered them a variety of fine liqueurs, but they were so full they hardly talked at all. For the first time in a week, Dr. Shatsky was able to relax and enjoy the luxury around him. He tried to imagine living like this day after day, year after year, but it seemed incredible to him. Finally, well after midnight, the doctor and the count arose and retired to the bedroom, where fresh nightclothes had been laid out for them. They drew the curtain between the beds, and Dr. Shatsky undressed and slipped under the covers. The starched white linen sheets felt luxurious, and the bed contained not a single lump—unlike his chaff-filled mattress at home, whose every hill and valley he knew by heart. The clacking of the wheels lulled him into a drowsy stupor, but every time he began to drift off he saw himself standing before the czar as he would tomorrow, and was jolted awake by the nervous clenching of his stomach.

The following morning Dr. Shatsky was awakened

by the shriek of the train's whistle and the appear-
ance of the white-jacketed waiter with a tray of tea
and freshly baked breads. He had only time to
dress hurriedly and gulp down a glass of tea before
the train pulled into Moscow station. A porter
helped him with his bag, and when he descended
from the carriage he saw that the train had pulled
onto a special siding, far from the noise and com-
motion of the public platforms. Count Vernichik
was already on the platform, and a royal carriage
stood nearby, its four snow-white horses ready to
carry them to the palace.

It was only a short drive, and Dr. Shatsky almost
wished it were longer. He hadn't seen the bustle of
a big city since he left Berlin many years ago, and
he was fascinated to see again the tall, broad public
buildings squatting in open squares like petrified
wedding cakes, and the well-dressed citizens hurry-
ing about on their errands. Most of all he was
amazed at the shapely and colorful domes of St.
Basel's Cathedral, which seemed to lift weightlessly
above the lead-colored streets like aspiring bal-
loons.

In no time at all they arrived at the palace. The
carriage rattled over cobblestones through a series
of yawning gateways, each of which was guarded
by a pair of tall, mustachioed Cossacks in uniform
with rifles on their shoulders and vicious-looking
scimitars hanging from their belts. They didn't look
at all like the half-wild murderers who pillaged the
ghettos, but still Dr. Shatsky shuddered and looked
away as they passed, for fear they would somehow

recognize him as a Jew. He felt as though he was being ushered right into the maw of the beast, and he regretted that he had ever come, that he hadn't fled the country at once when he heard that he would be summoned to the palace. He looked at the floor and tried to calm himself. If his urbane traveling companion, the count, noticed his discomfort, he gave no sign of it.

Finally they arrived at a broad marble portico, and the door of the carriage was opened by a footman whose red uniform was so crisply starched and pressed that it looked like it would crack in two as the footman made a deep bow. "Welcome, Count Vernichik; welcome, Dr. Shatsky," he said, though the doctor had not been introduced. "His highness awaits you within."

The footman led them deep into the palace, down hallways paved in colored marble and hung with rich tapestries, past glowing chandeliers and gleaming mirrors in gilt frames, to a private room so small that the doctor was startled when he realized that the man bent over the writing desk not three meters away was Czar Alexander II himself. The prized wolfhounds, of which the doctor had heard so much, were lounging on the floor around him. The footman withdrew, and the doctor and the count stood silently for a moment until the czar arose. He wore a fashionable uniform of strikingly pure white, its breast full of decorations and medals. As he faced them, his scowl melted into a welcoming smile.

"Count Vernichik," he beamed as he extended his

hand and the count bent to kiss the royal ring, "thank you for bringing our friend, Dr. Shatsky." And to the doctor he said, "Doctor, your reputation precedes you, and you are most welcome to our home." Dr. Shatsky smiled and nodded his head, but he did not bow or kiss the ring, for a Jew may not make obeisance to a worldly person, however high and mighty. Yet the czar seemed to take no offense. "We are grateful you have decided to assist us in this momentous event," he added, as though Dr. Shatsky had had a choice. "Come, the czarina is in her chambers, and the royal midwife is with her now. We would like your assurance that all is well."

The czar led the way down a short, unfurnished corridor quite in contrast with the splendid halls through which they had passed before, the wolf-hounds following at his heels and Dr. Shatsky and Count Vernichik bringing up the rear. Dr. Shatsky reflected with amazement on how unassuming the czar was in person, and he realized with surprise that the czar was, after all, only just a man. He was youngish, perhaps in his early thirties, tall, and very handsome. He sported only a moustache and sideburns, although many of the titled men of that day affected short, well-shaped beards. His most outstanding feature was his sparkling dark-brown eyes, which seemed to take in everything around him at a single glance. He seemed not to care at all that Dr. Shatsky was a Jew, although he must certainly have known. Indeed, this obviously very intelligent young man did not seem at all the kind of despot who commanded Cossacks and kept the entire population in fear of his wrath. He seemed more like a scholar, Dr. Shatsky thought, or a dignified gentleman of leisure. Did he share his subjects' disdain of Jews? The doctor couldn't imagine that such a man would succumb to blind prejudice. Perhaps he simply did not care, perhaps he simply thought Jews were unworthy of his concern. Whatever the czar's true feelings, he seemed polite enough. What Dr. Shatsky had seen of him so far was entirely incongruous with his reputation among the people.

The czar stopped before a heavy, carved door and knocked twice, then pushed the door wide. They entered a large and very ornate bedroom, redolent of exotic perfumes, with dark, coffered walls and a thick carpet of woven silk. Half a dozen beautiful women in flowing gowns dropped to their knees as the czar crossed the threshold with his wolfhounds, Dr. Shatsky, and Count Vernichik behind him. At the far end of the room was an enormous circular bed, and the woman reclining on its lace-trimmed pillows, a white wolfhound languidly lying by her side, could only be the czarina. Her beauty was stunning, even at first glance. Long ringlets of golden hair were piled luxuriantly on her head, and her blue eyes were wide and deep as the sea. Folds of diaphanous chiffon draped from her arm as she extended her hand to Dr. Shatsky.

"My dear," said the czar, "this is the famous Dr. Shatsky I have told you about, who will attend to the birth of our son. Dr. Shatsky, I present to you my wife, the Czarina Maria Alexandrovna."

"I am very pleased to make your acquaintance," said Dr. Shatsky in his very best Russian as he took her hand. She said nothing, but smiled graciously at him.

"And this," said the czar, moving on to the eldest of the several other women in the room, "is the royal midwife, Madame Algana." She was a formidable woman, Dr. Shatsky could see as she rose from where she knelt and bowed slightly to him. Her hips and shoulders were broad as the beam of a ship, and her rugged face held a ruddy, robust beauty. "Madame Algana delivered the czar himself many years ago," the czar continued, and Dr. Shatsky realized that he was referring to himself. "And now she will attend the birth of his heir—under your supervision, Doctor, of course." It was not the custom in those days for males to assist directly with a delivery unless there were complications that required the expertise of a doctor. This had been no less true at the university hospital where Dr. Shatsky had studied than it was in the ghetto homes of Orsha, where Froy Mikeles, the local midwife, would only call Dr. Shatsky in the event of a complication. He assumed that, as usual, Madame Algana would perform the actual delivery while he stood by, ready to take over if need be, and the czar's words confirmed his assumption.

"You may begin your examination, Doctor," said the czar, adding "I'm sure Madame Algana can tell you all you need to know." It seemed he was not to examine the czarina directly, but through the medium of the midwife. But while he asked the midwife about the czarina's health and comfort, he looked over at the czarina to see what he could deduce. She looked very healthy, indeed, just as the midwife affirmed. He abdomen was huge, and she was obviously well into the third trimester of pregnancy. Dr. Shatsky was pleased to see that her hips seemed strong and amply wide to accommodate the birth, and that her breasts had already begun to swell. He asked the midwife when her highness had last menstruated, hoping that the question would not embarrass the royal couple, who listened intently to every word. But it did not seem to bother them at all, and so the doctor proceeded to ask whether the czarina suffered from morning sickness, to which Madame Algana answered that she had, but that it had disappeared some weeks ago.

Then the doctor turned to the czar. "Majesty, you should be very proud. Her highness is in excellent condition, and the royal pregnancy is progressing very well. You may expect delivery in about six weeks, perhaps slightly more or less. But if your highness will allow, I would like to make an examination by stethoscope."

The czar seemed surprised and arched an eyebrow, but he clapped his hands and a servant, whom Dr. Shatsky had not noticed before, ran to fetch a stethoscope. The instrument he brought was of solid silver, unlike the doctor's own, which was wooden; but like all stethoscopes of the day it was simply a hollow tube about six centimeters long, with a flange at either end. Some models had a diaphragm of gut on the business end, but the doctor was glad to see this one did not, for he felt he could hear the tiny beating of a fetal heart better without it. He dared not ask the czarina to undress, but carefully placed one end of the stethoscope against the gown over her abdomen, apologizing for the familiarity. Now that he looked a little closer, he saw that she had indeed grown very large, and he wondered if she might not be carrying twins. As the czar looked on with intense curiosity, Dr. Shatsky nestled his ear in the other end and listened carefully. Immediately he heard the small but firm beating of the heart of the royal fetus. It was fast and strong, just as it should be, but he was unable to tell whether he heard two tiny hearts or only one.

"It sounds very fine," he said, straightening. "Your child will have the heart of a lion." The czar and the czarina beamed. They seemed amazed that the doctor could really hear the heart of their unborn child. Seeing the czar's eagerness, Dr. Shatsky offered, "Would your majesty also like to hear the heartbeat of his child?"

"Yes, we would," said the czar imperiously. Dr. Shatsky again placed the stethoscope over the czarina's abdomen, and the czar bent to listen. At first he said nothing, then he scowled. "I hear nothing," he said sternly. Dr. Shatsky listened again and moved the stethoscope slightly until the beating came loud and clear, then invited the czar to listen again.

This time the czar held his ear to the tube for a

long moment in rapt attention, and when he stood up his face glowed with exultant pride and obvious awe before the creation of new life. In his joy, he looked no different than any other proud father that Dr. Shatsky had ever seen, but what he said was in a class by itself.

"It is a miracle!" he proclaimed. "We have heard the heartbeat of the future of Russia, and it is certainly the heartbeat of a wise and strong ruler." Doctor Shatsky did not disabuse him of his certainty that the child would be a boy.

"We have a most excellent physician to attend our royal birth," the czar concluded. "Dr. Shatsky, you may retire now. We shall summon you when your services are needed."

With that the czar turned and strode out of the room, and the ladies-in-waiting returned to their business.

"Come," said Count Vernichik. "I'll show you to your rooms." He led Dr. Shatsky down the plain corridor along which they had come to a broad door not far away, and ushered him into a spacious room furnished with lavishly upholstered chairs, a fringed divan, and an enormous canopied bed. On either side of the room, doors opened onto a bathroom and a dressing room. "You may take your ease here," he instructed. "A page will call for you when you are needed." And with that he left the doctor alone. Except for the few hours he had slept on the train, it was the first time he had been alone since the previous morning.

The doctor stood for several minutes in the

middle of the room and looked around. He couldn't believe that this room, larger than his entire house in the ghetto, was meant for him and him alone. But now he began to wonder. Was he to wait here until the czarina was ready to deliver? Apparently so, although it would certainly be several weeks. He had supposed they would permit him to return to Orsha until the czarina's time drew near, but now he began to doubt. He was relieved that he had passed his first interview; in fact, it seemed he had made a very good impression. Fortunately, no one had said a word about his religion—so far, at least. But still he had no way of knowing the czar's real intent.

For the next five weeks the ghetto doctor was like a prisoner in the lap of luxury. Every morning he was called to examine the czarina, but her pregnancy progressed exactly as it should, and there was nothing remarkable about it except the enormous size to which her belly had grown. It must be twins, he thought, and he prayed it was; for if it were a single baby so large, the delivery would certainly be difficult.

The rest of the time he was as idle as a broken watch in a drawer, for it was made clear to him that under no circumstances was he to leave the palace. Three times each day a white-coated waiter like the one on the train wheeled in a cart of the most elaborate cuisine Dr. Shatsky could imagine, including caviar, truffles, and fresh vegetables that he knew were not yet in season, and he ate whatever seemed not to be too trayf. In the afternoons he often played chess with Count Vernichik, who beat him handily every time but taught him some rudimentary strategies, and after a while the two became almost friends. Evenings he read Russian literature from the many books that lined one wall of his room, and tried to occupy his mind as best he could. For he knew that if he let his mind wander he would worry about his patients in Orsha, whom he had left in care of Dr. Selkov, the town doctor. And he would become desperately homesick for his wife and children and his own little house in the ghetto. Saturdays were the most difficult of all. They seemed to strech out in endless langor. He prayed almost all day long, but whenever he took a rest from his devotion he would become intensely lonely. He wished more than anything to be back home in Orsha celebrating the shabbes with his family, or at a service conducted by Rabbi Shmul at the humble ghetto shul.

Then one day Dr. Shatsky was amazed to find something on his plate that he hadn't even dared to dream of, something so simple and wonderful that it brought tears to his eyes. Blintzes! Delicious cheese-filled blintzes, smothered in rich cream and topped with an elegant thimbleful of shiny black caviar, steam rising from them with an aroma that seemed to have been bottled in heaven itself. So, he thought, the word was out! Apparently the royal household was prepared to tolerate a Jew under their roof—at least while they had a use for him. He gave a prayer of deep gratitude to G-d for protecting him in the czar's palace, just as He had protected Daniel in the lion's den. Then he fell upon those blintzes like a ravenous wolf. He'd never tasted anything so delicious in all his life, and he relished every savory bite. But when he had finally scooped the last morsel from the plate, a sudden despondency settled over the doctor like a shroud. Would he never see his home again?

And so it went, week after endless week. As the first of March approached, Dr. Shatsky ordered the instruments he might need to assist in a complicated delivery. He wrote out the list and gave it to a page; fortunately the page couldn't read and had no idea what was on the list, and the doctor was glad that no one seemed to know he had ordered scalpels and sutures just in case; he hated to think how they'd react if they thought he was even thinking of cutting open the czarina! He also ordered carbolic acid to sterilize the instruments, and basins in which to soak them. The very next day everything was provided in double the quantities he had ordered. Clearly the czar would omit no possible precaution.

Finally one afternoon a page came to Dr. Shatsky's room, his eyes wide and his voice urgent. "Doctor!" he cried. "You must come immediately. It is time."

Dr. Shatsky snatched up his prized forceps and hurried to the boudoir of the czarina. The entire room was in pandemonium. The czarina lay on her bed gasping and moaning. Her labor had already begun. Madame Algana and several ladies-in-waiting anxiously mopped her brow and fluffed her pillows, which was all they could do for her. The czar stood a few meters away watching all this frantic activity, the very picture of a nervous first-time father, just as Dr. Shatsky himself had been at the birth of his own first son. At his feet, several wolfhounds whined nervously as they looked on uncomprehending.

Despite the uproar, everything seemed to be in order. The instruments he had ordered were soaking in the carbolic acid, and Dr. Shatsky dropped his obstetrical forceps in with them. The czarina's contractions, though strong, were still ten minutes apart, and there was still time for some final preparations.

The only thing that concerned Dr. Shatsky was the dogs in the room. Acquainted as he was with the new theories of bacterial infection and contagion, the doctor could not allow animals in the delivery room. But it would be a delicate task to ask the nervous czar to banish his cherished pets. Screwing up his courage, Dr. Shatsky took Czar Alexander aside and explained the situation as tactfully as he could.

At first the czar was indignant. "Do you mean to tell us," he retorted, "that the royal wolfhounds are not good enough to attend the birth of the next czar of Russia? How dare you! Our dogs accompany us everywhere—they are our royal mascots. And Dasha, her imperial majesty's dog, even sleeps with her at night, and she is very, very unhappy whenever she is away from her highness. So how can you say that they must be banished from these chambers?"

In a quiet voice that he hoped would calm the ruler, Dr. Shatsky explained in some detail that infection was spread by bacteria, which accumulated on all organic matter. That was why the instruments had been treated with carbolic acid, he explained, and why the shedding hair of dogs—royal mascots or not—posed a distinct danger to the welfare of both mother and child.

"Are you saying our dogs are dirty?" demanded the czar.

"No, no, majesty, not at all," Dr. Shatsky hastened to reassure him. "But germs are everywhere, and we cannot take any chance on such an important occasion." The last argument seemed to sway the czar, but just to make sure, Dr. Shatsky played his trump card: "This is how my teacher, Professor Himmelsdorf, instructed me."

"Very well, then," agreed the czar reluctantly. He clapped his hands and a page came and led the whining hounds out of the room.

Meanwhile the czarina's labor had intensified, and she was now crying loudly and asking for relief. When the czar heard this he became alarmed, and demanded that the doctor give her a dose of laudanum, a common opiate of that era. Dr. Shatsky knew from experience that giving laudanum too early might stop the labor, and giving too much of it might render the newborn sleepy and make it difficult to start the baby's breathing. Yet he dared not contradict a direct order of the czar. The czar had been remarkably tolerant of him so far, but Dr. Shatsky didn't want to push his luck. Fortunately Madame Algana, who had delivered the czar herself and who therefore had some amount of influence over him, also understood the dangers of giving laudanum during the early part of labor, and she and the doctor encouraged the czarina to be strong and patient. Finally, when the contractions were almost continuous, Dr. Shatsky prepared a small syringe and gave the czarina a mild dose, and he was happy to see that her suffering was reduced almost immediately.

Dr. Shatsky took up the stethoscope, which had been placed near at hand, and listened again at the czarina's abdomen, which he now insisted be exposed. He located the heartbeat, and was glad to hear that it was still pulsing steadily despite the laudanum and the contracting uterus. But he still could not be sure whether there were one or two heartbeats.

"How is it?" demanded the nerve-wracked czar at his elbow. "Can you still hear his heart?"

"Yes, of course," answered the doctor. "Everything is fine. Hear for yourself."

The czar bent over the stethoscope and relaxed visibly when he heard the baby's beating heart. But just then the czarina was seized with another contraction, and, as is usual, the beating could not be heard. The czar was terror-stricken. "What has happened? What has happened?" he asked over and over again.

"Don't worry, majesty," Dr. Shatsky reassured him. "It's quite normal." When the contraction had stopped, he let the czar listen again, and the ruler was relieved when he heard the beating heart again, and his confidence in Dr. Shatsky was restored.

"Everything is going to be just fine," said Dr. Shatsky. "But it's likely to be a while before her highness delivers, maybe an hour or more. Perhaps you would like to relax in the anteroom?" If there was one thing experience had taught him, it was how much more helpful a nervous father could be if he were absent.

"Yes, that's a good idea," said the czar. "But you call me the moment something happens."

The czar left the room and two court physicians came in. One of them was short and stout, and carried a bottle of chloroform, which Dr. Shatsky asked him to put aside until the delivery began. The other was tall, lean to the point of lankiness, and wore a blank expression on his face. They all gathered around the bedside and waited while Madame Algana held the czarina's hand.

It was a long labor, though not unduly so, Dr. Shatsky thought. A sumptuous meal was brought in, and Dr. Shatsky ate what little he could; the court physicians, however, greedily gobbled everything that was put in front of them, and everything Dr. Shatsky left, as well. Obviously they were not ordinarily fed as well as Dr. Shatsky had been during his five-week internment.

Finally, Madame Algana gave the report they

were all waiting for. "It's time," she said. "She's beginning to open up."

The royal doctors snapped to attention, and Dr. Shatsky asked the corpulent one to stand by with the chloroform. The czarina's contractions grew stronger and her pain more severe as she bore down, unimpeded by the laudanum. It was time for the chloroform to be started. Dr. Shatsky admonished the court physicians, "Please give very little chloroform until I tell you she is ready to go to sleep." The delivery progressed quickly from that point, and in a moment Dr. Shatsky signaled the other doctors to put the czarina to sleep. And then, as easily as if she were passing wind, the czarina delivered first the head, then the shoulders, then the hips, and finally the legs of the firstborn child of the royal family.

It was a girl, they all saw at once. Madame Algana cut and tied the umbilical cord and laid the crying infant on the bed beside her mother. Dr. Shatsky listened carefully to the baby's breathing and heartbeat, which seemed perfect and miraculously beautiful. His joy was only slightly mitigated by the thought that the czar might be disappointed that his child was not the boy he had been expecting.

But when Dr. Shatsky returned his attention to the czarina he saw that her belly was still quite full. Instantly he knew his suspicions had been correct: there would be not one baby, but two. He warned the midwife to watch for a twin and instructed the other doctors to reduce the chloroform so that the second baby would not be sleepy, and in almost no time at all the czarina delivered a second baby girl, as beautiful and as perfect as the first, and as alike as another pea from the same pod. Dr. Shatsky was thrilled as he examined the second baby; no matter how many births he attended, the miraculous event never ceased to move him to his very soul. Perhaps, he thought, the czar's disappointment would be lessened when he saw how beautiful his twin daughters were, and with that thought he dispatched one of the court physicians to fetch the czar.

Just as Dr. Shatsky finished his examination of the second baby and Madame Algana finished sponge-bathing the czarina and pulled the blankets up over her, the czar strode into the room. Dr. Shatsky saw at once the radiant glow on his face and knew immediately that the ruler was not at all disappointed. But the doctor was amazed when the czar walked right up to him and embraced him in a big bear hug! Who could imagine that Alexander himself, czar of the Russian empire, would hug a Jewish doctor from the ghetto! But at that moment there were no Jews and no Russians, no ruler and subject, but only a proud, happy father and the doctor who had supervised the delivery of his children.

"Congratulations, your majesty," said Dr. Shatsky, not knowing what else to say.

"Thank you, Doctor," replied the czar in genuine gratitude. "You have done a wonderful job. And now—let me see my little girls!"

Late that night Dr. Shatsky returned to his room, tired as a fisherman after an all-night trip. He fell across the bed without even undressing, and in less than a minute he was sound asleep. When he awoke the next morning the sun was already high in the sky. Birds were singing joyfully in the trees outside the window, and from down the hall came the sound of a newborn baby crying. The doctor felt refreshed, if a bit limp. All he'd done was stand by and watch, he told himself, but his body had a different opinion. The suspense and stress of the royal birth had taken their toll on him, and he fell back onto the pillow and slept until well into the afternoon. When he awoke again he found a covered silver tray with his dinner already waiting on the table, and when he lifted the lid what he found made him laugh out loud: blintzes again!

Dr. Shatsky remained at the palace for two more days at the czar's insistence, to make sure that mother and daughters were in good condition, although he protested that he had no particular qualification as a pediatrician. Each day he made several visits to the czarina, who was resting very comfortably with her sybaritic wolfhound again at her side, and twice daily he examined the twins, both of whom were doing splendidly. Otherwise, those days consisted of long hours of much-needed rest and meals that he barely picked at, and they passed without incident—except that Dr. Shatsky finally managed to force Count Vernichik into a stalemate in their final game of chess.

At last, on the third morning after the royal birth, Count Vernichik appeared at the door to tell Dr. Shatsky that he might leave today, and that he was ready to take him by carriage to the royal train, which waited at his disposal in the station. Dr. Shatsky didn't have to be asked twice. In less than an hour his small bag was packed and he was ready to go.

But there was one more surprise yet to come, for just as Dr. Shatsky was about to leave his room, Czar Alexander appeared in the doorway, smiling broadly.

"We must thank you again, Doctor," said the czar. "You have performed a great service not only for us, but for Mother Russia as well." He handed the doctor a small leather pouch of golden ten-ruble coins, saying, "Please accept this as a small token of our appreciation. And I shall send a letter to Professor Himmelsdorf thanking him for recommending so competent a physician to us."

Doctor Shatsky couldn't believe his ears. "Your highness," he replied, "I must say that the pleasure has truly been my own. I hope you will let me know if I can ever be of service to the royal household again."

Count Vernichik drove Dr. Shatsky to the station and saw him aboard the train. He was the only passenger on the long journey back to Orsha, and he felt more than a little ashamed by the luxury that surrounded him. That evening the chef prepared the same extravagant quantities of food as before, and it broke the doctor's heart to leave nearly all of it untouched, especially when he thought of the many poor people back home in Orsha.

That night he slept like a baby, and when he awoke the train was already standing in the Orsha station, where a few cabs and horses loitered about the platform. The doctor took up his old, frayed suitcase and stepped down into the sunlight. He was home again at last, he thought gladly, and suddenly his adventure of the last five weeks seemed like nothing more than a dream.

When Dr. Shatsky got home, his wife wept to see that he was still alive and well. She cooked up a simple meal of borscht and salt fish, which was even more delicious to him than any of the royal chef's most exotic recipes.

Then the doctor went to call on Rabbi Shmul, and told him all that had transpired. He gave the rabbi the bag of golden coins the czar had given him, asking that the rabbi see that the money was given to the needy families of the ghetto. He himself had no desire to keep the money; the memory of his time at the royal palace was all the reward he required.

But when he returned home again, Dr. Shatsky discovered a souvenir that had followed him home without his knowing it. On the shoulder of his coat he found a long, dark-brown hair, and with a start he realized that it must have fallen from the head of the czar when he embraced him in the czarina's bedchamber after the royal birth!

The doctor held the hair in the light and admired its shine, reflecting as if from that place and time which now seemed so far away. Dr. Shatsky carefully placed the czar's hair between the pages of his diary, and for the rest of his life he cherished this memento of the time the czar of Russia had embraced a poor Jewish doctor from the ghetto.

The Miraculous Milk Cow

REB MASHA AND his wife Rachel-Shemel were among
the poorest people in the ghetto. Masha worked as
an assistant to Reb Musskala, the cobbler, and
spent his days sewing new soles and nailing new
heels onto shoes that had already been repaired
over and over again. They lived simply in a little
house on the edge of the ghetto, and their most
valuable possession was a milk cow that Rachel's
father had given them as a wedding present. Her
father was long gone—as was the rest of their families. But the cow, whom they named Dvina, continued to give them fresh milk for their three-year-old

daughter, Ala, and sometimes a few liters extra to sell to a local dairy. It brought them only a few rubles each month, but they depended on that little extra to supplement Reb Masha's meager income, and they needed it in order to survive. Somehow they got by, and they never complained. In fact, the few times Rabbi Shmul tried to help them, Masha and Rachel gratefully declined his charity. They were doing all right, they insisted.

But then came a stroke of bad luck, a simple thing that meant disaster for the little family. The cow died.

Bad luck brings hardship to any family, but if a family has a dependable income, it can still carry on as before. But when tsouris befall a poor family like Reb Masha's and Rachel-Shemel's, they become tragedies that disrupt the family's entire way of life.

And so, when their milk cow died without warning, it was a real catastrophe. One evening she just didn't show up for milking, and when Reb Masha walked out to the pasture he found her lying stiff and cold on the grass. There lay his family's security and future, he thought, without a breath of life or hope left.

Reb Masha went back to the house and told Rachel-Shemel what had happened, and for a long while they stood there in the kitchen in despondent silence. "We'll have to get a new cow, somehow," she said.

"Maybe we could butcher the old cow and sell the meat," he suggested.

"I don't think that would be kosher," she said.

They stared at the floor for a minute. Then she said, "You know, I heard that Dr. Shatsky gave Rabbi Shmul some money that the czar paid him for delivering the royal twins last month, and that Rabbi Shmul was to use the money to help the poor. Maybe we could borrow enough to buy another cow."

"Na," said her husband, "how would we ever pay it back?"

"I don't like to take charity any more than you do," she said at last, "but this time I don't think we have any choice."

So that very evening they reluctantly knocked on the door of my great-great-grandfather's house, and Helga showed them in.

"Welcome," said Grandpa as he rose from the table at which he'd been studying the Talmud. "I've heard about your cow, and I'm so sorry. I hope you're getting along okay?"

"Well," began Reb Masha hesitantly, "that's why we're here. You know, it's very difficult for us to lose the cow. Without the milk she gives us for our little girl, and the little extra we have to sell, I don't know how we'll get by. We'll have to replace her somehow, but we don't have a kopek to spare right now."

"Hmm," said the rabbi. "That is a problem." He thought immediately of the money Dr. Shatsky had given him, but he knew the couple didn't like to be offered charity.

"Well, rabbi, we did have one idea," said Rachel-

Shemel. "I know that animals that have died are not usually kosher. But our cow died of old age, not disease; she was healthy as could be, then all of a sudden, *phfth!* So can't we call the shochet to butcher the carcass for us? Then we could sell some of the meat and get enough cash to buy a calf, and we'd also have something to eat."

Rabbi Shmul was horrified. "Absolutely not," he insisted. "No animal that has not been killed by a shochet according to the laws of koshreth may be eaten. Not even if it committed suicide."

Reb Masha and Rachel-Shemel were disappointed, but not surprised. "Well," Reb Masha said, "that doesn't leave us much choice. We've heard that Dr. Shatsky gave you the money he got from the czar to give to the poor. Would it be possible for us to borrow enough to buy a new cow?"

"Yes, that's true," said Shmul eagerly, "and you're more than welcome to it. How much do you think you'll need?"

"I…I really have no idea," mumbled Reb Masha, somewhat embarrassed. "We've never bought a cow before."

"No matter, not to worry," said Rabbi Shmul as he reached into the back of a cupboard and pulled out the sack of coins the czar had given Dr. Shatsky. "I'll give you three golden ten-ruble coins—thirty rubles all together. That should be more than enough, don't you think?"

"W-why, yes, Rabbi. I think so," stammered Reb Masha as he accepted the loan. He'd never held so much money in his hands before.

"And you needn't be concerned about paying it back," said my great-great-grandfather. "Dr. Shatsky wanted the money to be given to people who need it. All you have to do is thank him sometime. But if the cow costs less, please return the balance so that some other family can have it."

"Thank you, Rabbi," said Reb Masha and Rachel-Shemel together. But then a new problem occurred to them, and Rachel-Shemel was obviously embarrassed as she said, "But I'm afraid we don't even know where to buy a cow. Can you help us find one?"

"Well," answered the rabbi, "I'm not sure, but I've heard that the dairy in Limilik often sells cows. It's only three kilometers away; why don't you ask there?"

"Um...but isn't that on the other side of the Enchanted Forest?" asked Reb Masha.

"Yes, but don't worry," said the rabbi. "I've been there recently myself, and there's really nothing to be afraid of."

"We'll try," said Rachel-Shemel, pluckier than her husband because she had no intention of accompanying him on the buying trip.

The next morning Reb Masha set out on the road to Limilik. It was a beautiful day in early spring and a rare chance for him to get out of the ghetto for a few hours, and he enjoyed the walk immensely. After a while he came to the edge of the Enchanted Forest, and as he passed he heard a beautiful musical sound coming from the woods. He went to inves-

tigate and found that the sound came from a bab-
bling brook running clear and cold from newly
melted snow. Reb Masha wasn't used to walking so
far, and he was tired already. The banks of the
stream were covered with bright green grass and
dappled with sunlight, and Reb Masha lay down to
rest. In no time he fell asleep, and it wasn't until an
hour later that he awoke in a groggy haze. He
shook himself to clear his head and scolded himself
for falling asleep and losing time, then hurried on
to Limilik to complete his errand.

He had no trouble finding the dairy. At the edge
of the village stood an enormous sign, and although
Reb Masha couldn't read it, the life-size pictures of
cows were plain enough. He entered a bungalow
that looked like it might be the office, and was
greeted by a large woman who introduced herself
as Madame Ristokoss, the owner of the dairy. "How
can I serve you?" she asked.

Reb Masha was already nervous and confused.
"Well, you see, the other day our milk cow died. We
didn't even know she was sick...well, actually, she
wasn't sick, at least I don't think so...and I found
her in the field, and now we have no cow and no
milk and our daughter...."

"So you want to buy a milk cow?" interrupted
Madame Ristokoss, heading off what promised to
be an epic tale of woe. Reb Masha, tongue-tied,
nodded vigorously.

"Milk cows I have plenty," said the hefty woman.
"Come take a look."

She led Reb Masha out into the yard, then put

her fingers to her pursed lips and whistled so loudly Reb Masha jumped back. In a moment a dairyman in stained overalls brought up a beautiful cow for Masha's approval.

Reb Masha didn't know what to think. The cow was certainly pretty—a brown-and-white Guernsey with a white star on her forehead—but he wouldn't have known a good milk cow from one that was dry as a piece of matzo. "Her name's Reeva," said Madame Ristokoss, "and she gives lots of milk. D'you like her?" Reb Masha nodded even more vigorously than before. "She costs twenty rubles," said the woman, "and that's a bargain."

Reb Masha couldn't say a word, but he nodded again and reached into his pocket for the coins. He had a passing thought of offering less; he'd heard that you could bargain for things, and Rachel-Shemel had said that nobody ever paid the asking price. But he had never bought anything that cost more than a few kopeks, and he was afraid that if he offered less, Madame Ristokoss might be offended and withdraw her offer entirely. So he dug down deep and found first one then another coin; but instead of the third, he found a tattered hole at the bottom of his pocket.

His heart sank. "Vey is mir," he moaned to himself. "Why do poor men always have such tsouris?" It seemed like bad luck was following him from place to place.

But at least he had the two coins, and he paid them to Madame Ristokoss, who placed a rope around the cow's neck and handed it to Masha.

"Take good care of her," she said as he thanked her and said goodbye.

Masha and the cow headed slowly down the road, he dragging his feet with fatigue, and she trundling complacently along behind. By the time they reached the edge of the Enchanted Forest he was exhausted and needed to rest, so he tethered Reeva to a small tree on the banks of the little brook and let her graze while he lay down for a little nap. Reeva seemed quite content to graze in the fresh grass while her master rested; but Reb Masha couldn't sleep for worrying about the lost coin. Why do such things happen only to poor people, he thought? If I were a rich man it would be nothing to lose one little coin. But for me, it's a tragedy. What will I tell Rachel-Shemel? What will I tell Rabbi Shmul? Vey is mir, vey.... Finally he could stand it no more, and he got up and took Reeva home.

When she saw the cow, Rachel-Shemel fell in love with her immediately. "She's beautiful," she exclaimed. "She's young and strong, and I'm sure she'll give us lots of milk—maybe even more than Dvina did." Then she asked reluctantly, "So, how much did she cost?" When she heard the price she was appalled; but when she asked for the change and her husband just stared at the floor, she really hit the ceiling.

"Lost it? What do you mean, you lost it? Feh, Masha, you shlemiel, how could you lose ten rubles? Ten rubles, Masha; that's more than we make in a month! Oy, vey! What will the rabbi say?"

Fortunately my great-great-grandfather was not so hot tempered. "Not to worry," he said consolingly. "I was willing to give you all thirty rubles outright; if you still want to repay twenty someday, that's fine. Maybe the other coin will turn up somewhere."

❧

One morning about a week later, Rachel-Shemel sent Masha to check the fence along the back of their pasture, to be sure that it was still standing after a strong storm passed through and that Reeva hadn't kicked it down. He found the fence unbroken, and he noticed many flops of dung that showed that Reeva had been frequenting the back of the pasture. He was just about to go back to the house when his attention was arrested by something shining from one of the cow-pies. At first he thought it was the shiny tuchus of a bluebottle fly; but as he bent closer he could see that it was gold, not blue. He found a stick and dug into the dung, and lo and behold, there was the lost gold coin!

Reb Masha picked it up and wiped it off on the grass until it was as shiny as new. It must have fallen out of his pocket during his first rest stop at the brook; then, during the second stop, Reeva must have swallowed the coin while grazing on the grass. Reb Masha was overjoyed as he ran to show his find to his wife. He was so happy he didn't even hear her call him a shmendrick, but ran straight to the home of my great-great-grandfather, Rabbi Shmul.

Grandpa was happy and relieved to have the coin back. Not that the amount mattered at all; there were nearly a hundred rubles left in the bag, and one coin more or less didn't make much difference. But he was very glad that a burden had been lifted from his friend Reb Masha, who no longer felt bound to replace money he had never spent. And most of all the rabbi was glad that G-d—blessed be his holy name!—had watched over and protected a poor man, even if through the agency of a milk cow.

Miracles are not always spectacular things, my great-great-grandfather reflected after Reb Masha had gone. Oh, sometimes there are signs in the sky, voices from on high, and visions of a new Jerusalem. But other times, as is usual in the ghetto of Orsha, a miracle is no more than a golden glint in a pile of cow dung!